The Frannie Shoemaker Campground Series

Bats and Bones

The Blue Coyote

Peete and Repeat

The Lady of the Lake

To Cache a Killer

A Campy Christmas

The Space Invader

Real Actors, Not People

We Are NOT Buying a Camper! (prequel)

Also by Karen Musser Nortman

The Time Travel Trailer

Trailer on the Fly

Trailer, Get Your Kicks!

Happy Camper Tips and Recipes

Reunion and Revenge

The Mystery Sisters Book 1

by Karen Musser Nortman

Cover Art by Ace Book Covers

Copyright © 2018 by Karen Musser Nortman. All rights reserved. No part of this book may be reproduced in any form by any electronic or mechanical means (including photocopying, recording or information storage and retrieval) without permission in writing from the author.

This is a work of fiction. Names, characters, places and incidents are either the product of the author's imagination, or are used fictitiously, and any resemblance to actual persons, living or dead, business establishments, events, or locales is purely coincidental.

Dedicated to my 'younger aunts,' Carol Mast, Maxine Musser, and Lilian Jensen. You were our heroes and prime examples of strong, independent women.

Table of Contents

Chapter One	1
Chapter Two	11
Chapter Three	22
Chapter Four	31
Chapter Five	42
Chapter Six	55
Chapter Seven	65
Chapter Eight	74
Chapter Nine	82
Chapter Ten	90
Chapter Eleven	102
Chapter Twelve	114
Chapter Thirteen	124
Chapter Fourteen	133
Chapter Fifteen	141
Thank You...	152
Other Books by the Author	154
About the Author	159

Chapter One

Lillian Garrett shifted her bag of groceries to her purse arm and grabbed her mail from the barn-shaped mailbox on the gate post. Mostly junk mail, a couple of catalogs, and an envelope from Minnesota. That piqued her interest. Maybe from her sister Carol, who didn't write often.

Inside her neat Cape Cod, she headed for the kitchen and dumped everything on the counter. She opened the letter and pulled out a homemade flyer. It wasn't from Carol; Carol was a better speller.

JACOBSEN FAMILY RENUION

JUNE 22, 2018

THE BOB AND CAROL HARSTAD FARM
CASTLEROLL, MN

Friday night: Potluck Supper.
Bring table servise and one dish to share. Meat provided.

> Saurday morning: Castleroll Midsummer Parade, 9 am, Main street
> Saturday afternoon, 1 pm—Tour of old Jacobsen Antenna plant and Castleroll High School
> Saturday evening, 5:30 pm—catered dinner at the Castleroll VFW
> Sunday morning, 10 am—church services at St. John Lutheran Church
> Sunday noon—Midsummer Picnic in the Park (tickets available $10 per person)
> RSVP to Annie Harstad-Hansen by May 1

Lil called her older sister Maxine in Denver. "Max? Did you get Annie's invitation to the family reunion?"

"I haven't picked up my mail yet today. And how are you?"

Lil was used to ignoring her sister's sarcasm. After all, she'd had over seventy years of practice. "Fine, fine. Well, if you can believe it, they're getting up a reunion for the weekend of June 15."

"Castleroll?" Max asked.

"Yes. Bob and Carol's. Well, part of it anyway. I haven't been back there for years."

"Annie's wedding, I think, was the last time we went."

Lil shuddered. "Not a pleasant memory. I mean, the wedding was fine, but some of the guests weren't very friendly."

"'Some wounds run too deep for the healing.'"

"Who's that—Shakespeare?"

Max laughed. "Harry Potter—J. K. Rowling. So are you thinking about going to this shindig?"

"I want to. It would be a chance to see a lot of people in the family who don't really have room for us to come visit. For one thing, I'm worried about Sharon's granddaughter, Chelsea, and the trouble she's gotten into. Someone needs to talk some sense into her, and you know it won't be Sharon. I wonder how Carol's doing after her surgery. And it would be a good chance to decide what to do with Dad's memorial money. It's been three years."

"Good points. Listen, let me check my calendar and get my mail. I'll call you back tonight."

"Sure," Lil said. "I have to put my groceries away, anyway. Call me after 7:00 because I have dance class at 5:00."

"Dance class? Are you kidding?"

"Nope. I'm taking a tap dance class. Always wanted to."

"You'll break your leg. Talk to you later." Max was gone.

Max called back that evening. "Looks—um—interesting. But I thought you wanted to go to Pennsylvania this summer to see Terry and his kids."

"We could do that this fall. You don't sound very fired up."

"Actually, I am. I know how to handle those people now. It just took me by surprise at the wedding."

"Most of the people who worked for Dad are retired now, one way or another. Surely they aren't still mad at us. I can drive."

"Like I have a death wish. We'll make a time table later, but I'll swing down and pick you up. Maybe go a little early and make some stops along the way."

LATER, LIL WONDERED what Max meant by 'handling' people. Their father, George Jacobsen, had owned an antenna manufacturing company headquartered in Castleroll. It thrived during the Fifties and Sixties, but faltered in the Seventies as cable television moved in. George sold the company in 1977 to a conglomerate, which then closed the plant and moved operations to Tennessee, leaving many Castleroll residents without jobs. Jacobsen Antennas had been the town's largest employer by far. By that time, Lil had long been married and moved to Kansas, and Max was a professor of botany in a Colorado small college.

When the sisters returned to their hometown ten years earlier for their niece Annie's wedding—about thirty years after the plant closing—guests' reactions ranged from quiet snubbing to outright insults. Why would those people come to the wedding if they were still mad at the family? Just for the free food and drinks? It boggled the mind. Lil asked Carol afterwards how she could stand to stay in the area. Carol admitted that she stayed in her husband's shadow and made sure to strengthen her connections with his family whenever possible.

"Besides, our close friends don't blame me at all."

"As they shouldn't," Max had said. "None of us were involved in the company."

"They don't blame you. Most people have put it behind them. It's the people who don't know us well and were really hurt by the closing who can't let it go. It's just that so many of the family being in town for this wedding has reminded people."

OVER THE NEXT couple of months, LIL AND MAX planned their trip back to Minnesota for the reunion. Their nephew Grant, their brother Donnie's son, lived in Grand Island, Nebraska, so they would make an overnight stop there. Max called Grant and reported to Lil that he had no plans to go to the reunion.

"He said they'll be busy with summer softball. I asked about spending the night, and he said that their hide-abed has a broken spring, but I assured him we would be fine with all that."

"Good," Lil said. "I was sorry we missed him when we tried to stop last year on our Wisconsin trip. I didn't know someone that old could be in the National Guard. He must be fifty. Is he still doing that?"

"He didn't mention it."

"I'm putting together a scrapbook of family pictures to take along. I'm using a Disney theme."

"How appropriate," Max said.

Lil felt it was unfair and unnecessary sarcasm. Max never did appreciate Lil's creativity.

Lil scheduled a mani-pedi and a touchup on her blonde bouffant hairstyle for the week before the trip. After several shopping expeditions, she found the perfect matching lavender shirt and pants for the Friday night potluck. Lightweight—Minnesota summers could be hot—but some protection against the giant mosquitos. She had a cute denim jumper that would be great for the Saturday events, and still needed to make a decision on her Sunday clothes.

She loved planning for trips. She and her husband Earl travelled often during their marriage, but he had died from cancer eighteen years before. For a while she moped around home until Max suggested a road trip to the Carolinas.

For many people, that trip would have been the last time they ever traveled with Maxine. Max was the oldest of Lil's siblings—headstrong and bossy. They fought most of the trip. But by the time they returned home, Lil realized she felt more alive than any time since Earl died. At that point, she decided that these trips were doable if she just ignored Max's most annoying habits. Lil did love her sister, even if she often didn't like her much. So they still took trips, they still argued, and most of the time, Lil was able to blow off Max's comments. Most of the time.

THE SECOND WEEK in June, Max pulled in to Lil's driveway in her 1950 Studebaker Starlight coupe—bright red. Max bought the car when she retired and had it pristinely restored. The sisters used it for jaunts around the country to visit friends and family.

Max opened her door and was nearly flattened as a hairy, red projectile burst from the back seat. "Rosie!" Max shouted.

The 70-pound Irish Setter bounded to Lil, and leaped up, paws on Lil's shoulders and tongue hanging in her face. It was all Lil could do to keep her balance, but she laughed with delight. She gently removed Rosie's paws and let her down to the ground, scratching the dog's head. "I'm glad to see you, too, girl."

Max emerged from the car, brushed back her short gray hair, and straightened her brown tunic top. Lil thought she needed to wear more color, but Max stubbornly stuck with her neutral classics. She always said she was too old for 'fads.'

Lil hugged her sister. "Come in and take a short break before we leave. I have iced tea and fresh snickerdoodles."

"I do need to use the bathroom. Rosie! Come on!"

The dog was burrowing under a bush along the driveway. Max shook her head. "The only reason that dog is still alive is that she's beautiful. I swear she doesn't have a brain in her head."

"She's very friendly, too," Lil pointed out. "That's a plus."

"Oh, don't I know. Her friendliness is why half my neighborhood would like to see me evicted."

A half-hour later, Lil placed her rolling suitcase and matching tote in the large trunk next to Max's beat-up duffel bag. She smiled to herself at Max's refusal to give up anything that had even a modicum of use left. Max traveled often and could well afford a matched set of luggage but clung to her old duffel.

From Kansas, they headed north to Interstate 80 and then east toward Grand Island. Rosie had the entire back seat, and after trying to pace in the confined space the first ten minutes and bestowing her hot breath on the women, she finally collapsed on the seat and went to sleep.

"I wonder what our reception will be in town," Lil said, when things quieted down. "Is Donnie coming?"

Max grimaced. "Annie says he is. I just hope he doesn't stir things up. He's never been willing to let the past go either."

Grant and his wife welcomed them warmly, if not over-enthusiastically. The hide-a-bed was certainly lacking in creature comforts, but the women made it through the night.

When they discussed the reunion at supper, Grant said, "We are busy with the kids' activities, but truth be told, I have no desire to go back there. I never lived there, and people were so rude when we went to Annie's wedding. I had nothing to do with Jacobsen Antenna—it closed before I was born."

Lil patted his hand. "I know, dear. They are rather unfair about it."

"*Rather* unfair? That's pretty mild, Aunt Lil. Besides, my dad gets so mad when the subject comes up that we really don't want to be around him."

As they left in the morning, Mrs. Grant (Lil could never remember her first name—Alicia or Alyssa or something?) said "Stop back any time." But she kept her hands behind her back. Perhaps her fingers were crossed.

Max suggested a stop at Lake Okoboji in Iowa on their way to Minnesota.

"Since we don't have any relatives in the area, I found a little local motel that isn't too expensive and allows pets."

And it was cheap, apparently because they weren't paying for a 'free' breakfast, cable TV, or clean sheets. Lil made sure her suitcase and shoes were off the floor in case some of the bugs decided to explore, although Rosie was good at chasing them back to their lairs.

As they left the next morning, Lil said, "At least when we get to Castleroll and stay with Carol, we can be assured of clean beds."

Max rolled her eyes. "It wasn't that bad. Sometimes I think you have OCD."

CASTLEROLL, MINNESOTA, WAS FOUNDED in the 1800s by German settlers and named, understandably,

Germantown. The Germans were soon outnumbered by the Norwegians and Swedes, who flooded in by the turn of the century. In reaction to the anti-German sentiment during World War I, the city council (two Janssens, a Hultberg, an Amundsen, and a Hermanson) decided to rechristen the town. Long meetings did not result in any kind of agreement until Nils Amundsen stated one Monday that he had been to so many potlucks over the weekend that they ought to name the town Casserole.

The idea, although intended as a joke, had a great deal of appeal. There was no other town by that name and it reflected the culture of the town rather than that of any particular group. Bjorn Hultberg, however, thought it would make them a laughing stock—why not call the town 'Blue Plate Special'?—and suggested that the spelling be changed to Castleroll to give the name a little more class. The choice was immensely popular with most of the citizens—Scandinavians, Germans, and even the Poles.

Chapter Two

Max and Lil recognized few of the business names on Castleroll's wide main street. Amid the one and two-story commercial buildings stood the movie theater they remembered, but it appeared to be closed.

Lil pointed out the corner where the JCPenney store had once been. "Remember, it had those pneumatic tubes that whisked money up to the mezzanine and returned with change? Those fascinated me."

"That wasn't here. That was in Prairie City."

"No, it was here."

"Your memory's gone," Max said.

Lil gave up and gazed out the window.

The El Dorado Cafe and the Rivas Beauty Salon indicated that Latino residents had joined the Scandinavians, Germans, and Poles. Max drove slowly down the street, relishing the heads turned in envy at the sight of her sporty car. Once through the downtown, she stepped on the gas and followed the main road out of town to their sister Carol's house.

A long, straight lane led back to Carol and Bob's prosperous farm that had been in Bob's family for three generations. Southern Minnesota prairie stretched out in all directions from the well-kept farmstead. The old farmhouse had stood since the first generation, although it had been updated numerous times. Carol had removed the paneling and shag carpet when she and Bob married and gone through at least four redos since then. The latest, Carol had told Max on the phone, was the trendy 'shabby chic.' Not exactly Max's cup of tea, but it evidently suited Carol.

As they pulled up in front of the path to the house, Carol came out sporting a wide smile and a walker. Her hip replacement the previous winter had developed several complications, resulting in more surgery.

"You're here!" she called. "And that adorable car is like a ray of sunshine."

Lil hurried up the path to greet her sister, who waited leaning on her walker. Max pulled their bags out of the trunk. She left Lil's fancy luggage on the ground and, lugging her duffle, went to hug Carol.

"How's the hip?" Lil asked. "You're getting around better than I thought you would be."

"Ha! I thought I'd be jumping hurdles by this summer. It's been a hassle but it's gradually improving." Carol beamed at them both. "I'm so glad you guys could make it! Everyone is excited to see you."

Max cocked one eyebrow at her. "*Everyone?*"

Carol chuckled. "Well.... Let's go in and put your things in your rooms. I need your help to get things ready for the potluck tonight. Annie organized most of this, but of course she had to work today. Bob's in the field, so you'll see him later."

Max snagged the regular guest room, decorated rather sedately in gray, beige, and pale yellow, while Lil drew the room usually reserved for the granddaughters. The Disney princess comforter alone would have been enough to nauseate Max.

They gathered in the kitchen, and Lil ordered Carol, "Give us jobs and the latest gossip."

Carol gave her a sideways glance. "Do you even remember anyone? It's been years since you've been here."

"Annie's wedding," Max said. "No way to forget the bad feeling about the plant closing."

Carol tied on a blue-checked apron and leaned on her walker with one hand while she pulled a large yellow bowl from the cupboard. "I'm afraid it's about to be stirred up again. For one thing, Dutch Schneider is working on his memoir."

"Good Lord," Max said. "Is he still running the paper?"

"No, he retired last year. A young kid, Charlie Gomar, bought the paper and is the editor, photographer, feature writer, and ad man."

"Is it still a biweekly?" Lil asked.

"Once a week — and he scrapes the bottom of the barrel to do that. It seems like half the paper is reprints from fifty years ago, seventy-five, a hundred — you know."

Lil folded her arms and leaned against the cupboard. "But Dutch and Dad were really close. He wouldn't write anything bad about us."

Carol continued to assemble a bowl of coleslaw. "I'm sure he doesn't want to. But this Gomar had an editorial a few months back accusing Dutch of suppressing documents saying that Dad had *two* offers for the company: one for less money but guaranteed to keep the Castleroll plant open, and one for more money and the buyer would relocate the plant. Dutch may feel he has to defend himself in his book."

Max took the bowl from Carol to put in the fridge. "Sit down, and just tell Lil and me what you want us to do. Dad always said that he didn't know the new owners planned to close the plant."

Carol nodded and sat. "That's what he said. I have no idea if anyone has seen these so-called documents." She turned to Lil. "There are two apple pies in the freezer on the back porch. Would you get those, please, and we'll put them in the oven."

"Will do. Even if that's true, it would have been sort of selfish of Dad, but not illegal. He had a right to accept the best offer." Lil stepped out on the small back porch and opened the freezer to retrieve the pies.

While she put them in the oven, the back door opened and Carol's husband, Bob, walked in. He was a tall, lanky Gary Cooper type with laughing eyes and skin leathered by years in the fields.

"Take your shoes off," Carol called to him. "I've already mopped the kitchen."

"What? You cleaned just for your *relatives*?" He gave Lil and Max a wink. "I'll wait until after my shower to give you a hug, ladies, but for now, welcome." He gave them his infectious grin and wiped the sweat off his brow.

"We'll accept that condition, Bob," Max said.

Carol snapped him with a dishtowel as he slipped through the kitchen, and then turned to her sisters.

"We need to get the tables ready, too. Max, on the top shelf of that cupboard are plastic table cloths, plates, and so on. You'll probably need the step stool." Carol pointed to one leaning in the corner.

Lil and Max hauled the tableware outside while Carol clumped behind them with her walker. They spent the next half hour covering picnic tables that had been arranged in a long line.

Lil paused to take in the high sailing clouds and the light breeze. "A beautiful day for this." She turned to Carol. "If things are heating up again about the plant closing, why did Annie want to do this reunion and, especially, why here in Castleroll?"

Carol sighed. "Annie has always been adamant that, the later generations had no part in the plant closing, and no rumors are going to run her out of town." She gave them a sheepish smile. "She's pretty stubborn. And she thinks I'm a coward for trying to avoid the subject and hiding behind Bob's family name."

Lil put her arm around Carol's shoulders. "Well, let's put it aside for now. At least we know it should be a friendly crowd tonight. Do you want us to set up serving tables?"

Carol gave direction from the patio "Yes, thanks. There're two long folding tables in the shed. I thought we'd put the food tables on the patio. There's a couple of outlets there for anything that needs plugging in.".

Bob came out to help, looking refreshed, and they busied themselves getting the rest of the setup done. They finally stood back to admire the results and congratulate each other. The patio was well shaded, and the aqua and yellow plaid tablecloths brightened the space. Max had organized a beverage table in one corner, although Carol squelched her suggestion that they order a keg.

By the time they finished, Annie had arrived with her husband and three young children in tow. Other cars pulled in and parked in an open field across from the house. Lawn chairs and foil-covered dishes emerged from trunks. Although Lil's son Terry could not make it from Pennsylvania, her daughter Georgiann arrived from the Cities where she played in the Minnesota Symphony.

"Mom!" Georgiann said. "When are you coming up for a concert? I sent you the fall schedule—did you get it?"

"Yes, yes, I did. Max and I are talking about going to see Terry in the early fall and we could swing back up this way on our way home. Do you have room for us in your new place?"

"We are?" Max said.

Lil waved off her question. "I mentioned it."

The fourth and youngest sister, Sharon, and her husband, Harold, arrived with their granddaughter Chelsea. Max took in Chelsea's face. She had been in and out of drug rehab, and she might be headed back. Soon.

"Are Ernie and Kim coming?" Lil asked Sharon.

"Yes, they're not far behind us." She lowered her voice and leaned over to Lil. "Chelsea's not getting along with them very well."

Lil nodded. The reason was obvious, and she didn't really blame Chelsea's parents. "How about your other boys?"

"They can't make it."

By the time they arranged the food on the serving table, family members were lined up on both sides. Mothers balanced extra plates for their young ones and older kids looked askance at the offerings.

Guests oohed and aahed over traditional dishes—green beans in mushroom soup topped by canned French fried onions, meat loaf, and Grandma Jacobsen's potato salad. Some picked at the roasted beet Greek salad and looked suspiciously at the squash and spinach lasagna, considered exotic entries at a Minnesota potluck, while others forged ahead and threw caution to the winds.

After supper, Max managed to get the group lined up for photos. Georgiann was a good amateur photographer and able to get some decent shots using a tripod and the timer on her camera.

They all cleaned up the food and rearranged chairs for visiting. Adults bounced infants, who alternated between being alarmed and consumed with giggles over that activity. Donnie Jacobsen's latest pyramid scheme and Harold and Sharon's condo in Florida were popular topics. Older children chased each other around the farmyard, ignoring admonishments from parents to finish their suppers and not run with sticks. Rosie was in her element, trying to keep up with the kids.

By the time the sun set, the adults had gathered on the patio, closer to the beverage table, the youngest children had been settled in makeshift sleeping arrangements, while the older ones played flashlight tag and something called 'midnight ghost.'

Lil caught up with Georgiann's love life and Max talked to Sharon about Chelsea's problems. They exchanged stories about their childhood years in Castleroll--each more embarrassing than the last.

The conversation finally turned to the topic uppermost in their minds. Max opened a beer and took an empty chair next to her brother Donnie. Donnie was the youngest and, with four older sisters, grew up spoiled, in Max's opinion.

"Carol tell you what Dutch Schneider's up to?" Donnie asked.

"You mean about his memoir?" Max asked.

"That ungrateful turd!" Donnie exploded. "Dad bailed him out a couple of times from his gambling debts. More than I got."

Max laughed. "Oh, Donnie, Dad bailed you out more than the rest of us put together."

He spluttered and his face flushed. "When I was a kid, yeah, but I missed out on some big financial deals later because he wouldn't back me."

"Maybe because they weren't good deals? He was a pretty sharp businessman."

"He never gave me a chance!"

Maxine decided to change the subject. Donnie was never going to admit that he was a major screwup. "Whatever. What do you hear about Dutch's memoir?"

"Just that he has memos showing that Dad could have sold the company for less money and kept it open. Bunch of crap."

"Carol said that's what the new owner of the paper claims. Does Dutch admit that he has these memos?"

Donnie shrugged, a little deflated. "Dunno."

Time to change the subject again. "We stopped at Grant's on our way here. They seem to be doing well. He says you and Janet don't get out there often. You should — the kids are growing up fast."

Donnie bristled. "I'm not retired like you. Can't afford to go gallivanting around the country."

Max sighed. She'd almost forgotten how annoying Donnie's whining could be. "Right. Where are you staying this weekend?"

"That dumpy motel in town. Georgiann is at Annie's and so are Sharon and Harold, Ernie and Kim, and their brat Chelsea. Carol's full up out here, so I didn't have much choice."

Max turned to Bob, who was sitting on her other side. "Where's a good place to pick up the local gossip?"

"During the day? The coffee shop where Benton Oil used to be. And Barney's on Fourth Street is popular."

"Might have to check it out."

Bob laughed. "Just don't get in any fist fights. We don't want to bail you out."

Not long after, people began to pack up food and kids to make their way home or to temporary quarters. They would meet the next morning to watch the Midsummer Parade through Main Street.

Donnie was having trouble navigating, and Carol ordered him to leave his truck at the farm and let Sharon drop him off at the motel. He was spoiled, but used to being directed by his sisters, so he meekly let Harold lead him to their car.

Max and Lil ordered Carol to sit down while they cleaned up the supper remnants.

Lil wiped down the kitchen counters. "I don't think there's any hope that Donnie will ever grow up."

"That's probably our fault as much as his," Carol said.

Max didn't agree. "At some point, he has to take responsibility for himself."

"I bet that's why Janet didn't come. She gets tired of taking care of him," Lil said.

"Call me hardhearted, but I think the only reason *he* came was to try to sell his real estate scheme or whatever it is."

Max collected the towels and took them in to the adjoining laundry room. When she returned, she called Rosie for one more trip outside. "Then I'm turning in. It's been a long day."

Chapter Three

Saturday morning, Max and Lil took their coffee out to the patio while Carol showered. The morning promised another beautiful day. They discussed the gathering the previous night. Max relayed all of Donnie's complaints, and Lil shared what she had picked up from their sister Sharon.

"That Chelsea—what a heartache. She just got out of rehab a week ago and Sharon is pretty sure she's using again."

"Sharon needs to get more involved," Max said. "Her parents have let that girl run wild, and they're in way over their heads."

"That's what I told her. I said—" Lil stopped and looked up as Carol came to the door. Max jumped up to help with the walker while Carol negotiated the two steps. She pulled her cell phone out of her robe pocket, and her usually tan face was as pale as the white blossoms on the mock orange bush blooming by the door.

Lil studied her face. "You're upset about something."

"They found Dutch Schneider dead this morning." Her voice cracked. "He was murdered."

"What?" Maxine sat forward in her chair, bumping the side table and spilling her coffee.

Lil said, "Oh, my heavens!"

Carol collapsed in another chair. She gripped the phone and just nodded at them.

Max regained a little of her equilibrium and mopped up her spill with her napkin. "Murdered? How?"

"Stabbed with something." Carol held up the phone. "Annie called and that's what she said: *stabbed with something*. It must not have been a knife." She shook her head, still trying to grasp the news. "They found him in the alley behind the newspaper office."

Max looked at Lil. "You don't suppose Donnie…" She couldn't finish.

"Donnie? What do you mean?" Carol asked.

Max repeated Donnie's comments about Dutch. "He was pretty drunk when he left here."

"That's why I had Sharon drop him at the motel." Carol looked around the corner of the house. "His truck's still here. But I don't believe for a minute that he would do that."

Max wasn't so sure but kept her opinions to herself, for once. "Dutch didn't have any family, did he?"

"Just a niece in the Cities."

Lil said, "Murder! Here in Castleroll? I can't believe it."

"I don't think there is much question," Carol said.

Max got up to clean up her coffee mess. "This will put a damper on the parade. I assume they'll still have it."

Carol nodded. "Yes, lots of people in town for it and investments in the floats. They'll go ahead. I'd better go get dressed, and then I'll fix us a light breakfast before we go to town."

"That isn't necessary," Lil protested.

Carol waved her off. "It's done. I made a coffee cake yesterday and there's fresh fruit left from last night. If you want more than that, you're on your own."

AFTER THEY DRESSED and shared their breakfast, Bob loaded lawn chairs and Carol's walker in the trunk of the Studebaker.

Max held out the keys to him. "If you quit drooling on the seats, I'll let you drive it to town."

"Can I? Can I?" Bob said in his best sixteen-year-old imitation.

Annie had earlier roped off an area for the family in front of the old drug store—now the Get Potted pottery shop. Just as they reached the area, a man pushed one of the stanchions out of the way and dropped the rope, kicking it out of the way. He looked up at them, surprised at first, and then frowned.

"You people don't run this town any more!" He stomped off.

The sisters looked at each other, and Lil moved the other stanchion and coiled up the rope. "A little late, but at least we won't antagonize anyone further. Do you know that guy?" she said to Carol.

"Cecil Ridley. Does odd jobs around town. He hasn't had a regular job since the plant closed."

Annie arrived shortly, along with her kids, husband, and guests. Carol explained what had happened to the rope. Annie just grimaced and said, "Good Lord. What next?"

Confusion reigned while they set up and rearranged more chairs. Then they settled like a flock of birds.

Annie pulled her toddler onto her lap. "Anyone seen Donnie this morning?"

"His truck's still at my place, but we haven't seen him," Carol said.

Annie leaned forward after checking to see if anyone around them was listening. "The police came to our house looking for him."

"He's staying at the motel," Max said.

"That's what I told the cops, but they said he isn't there."

Max pushed a strand of gray hair behind her ear. "Maybe he went somewhere for breakfast. He still has a lot of buddies around here

"Probably trying to sell them his latest scheme." Carol grinned.

Annie's handsome husband, Dirk, laughed. "What is he selling, anyway? I avoided him last night."

"Some kind of wholesale marketing club, from what I understand," Bob said.

"Huh," Max said. "Shows you how much I listen to his blathering. I thought it was real estate or something."

As the start time neared, people spilled out from the sidewalk into the street, trying to get a glimpse of the first marchers. A deputy strode down the street urging the crowd back onto the sidewalk.

Max got up and dashed into the street, shading her eyes and peering down the street as if she was looking for the parade. As she stepped in front of the deputy, she twisted her ankle and started to go down. The deputy grabbed her arm and helped her to right herself.

"You all right, ma'am?"

"Yes, yes. Thank you."

He helped her hobble back to her chair. She thanked him again as she bent to rub her ankle.

"I'm sorry to take your time. I'm sure you're busy, looking for that murderer. We don't want anybody else to get shot, do we?" The deputy didn't notice Lil roll her eyes at Carol.

"Shot? No one was shot, ma'am. There was a man found dead this morning, but it looked like he was stabbed with part of a TV antenna." He shook his head at the folly of human beings—or at least murderers.

A drum cadence heralded the approach of the parade color guard. "I'd better go. You're sure you're okay?"

"Yes, thank you."

As he left, Carol leaned over and said, "This is going to get worse. And obviously our small town police department doesn't realize that they shouldn't be giving out that kind of information. How's your ankle? Do you want me to get your car?"

Lil scoffed. "She faked that in order to pump that poor officer. And you are the last one who should go get anybody's car." She patted Max's hand. "Good job of snooping. That antenna thing sounds like a frame job. I wish we knew where Donnie was."

"Did anyone try calling him?"

"He's not answering his phone," Carol said.

The color guard appeared, flags snapping. Two of the guard looked to be Korean or Vietnam War veterans and had difficulty keeping up, in step, and maintaining a military posture. The other three—two men and a woman—were younger and wore camo uniforms more typical of Afghan or Iraq war vets.

Units of the American Legion and the VFW followed with their own banners. Behind them, the Castleroll high school band in shorts and purple tee shirts struggled through the opening fanfare of "The Washington Post March." Spectators got to their feet, moved by the sentiment rather than the quality of the music.

"Wow," Max said. "I wish we could have worn shorts and tee shirts when we were in band."

"I don't know. I thought our uniforms were pretty sharp. All of that gold braid on the jackets and the stripe down the pants. Those outfits look kind of sloppy." Lil pointed at the last ranks of drummers.

Max scoffed. "Easy for you to say. You were a baton twirler and had a sleeveless top and short skirt. Those uniforms were hot."

Lil sighed and turned away to watch the line of hayracks, disguised with crepe paper and signs lettered with magic markers. One carried twenty or thirty dance students—all young girls in bright colored tutus and leotards. They resembled dolls with their overstated makeup, but they enthusiastically waved and threw candy into the crowd.

Another, sponsored by the local bank, featured bank staff dressed as forest sprites. Several other floats were designed by 4-H clubs and centered around the theme of summer fun with bicycles, kids in swimsuits, balloons, and one giant ice cream cone. The Lions, the Rotary, and other clubs and businesses had their own entries.

The last float held the Solstice Sweethearts: five young women wearing flower crowns and flowing pastel gowns. Fresh cut branches formed a canopy over them as they smiled, waved, and threw candy to the crowd. Following the floats, huge tractors, combines, cement mixers, and other massive machinery lumbered down the street. The drivers, too, threw candy, causing children to scamper into the street.

The last entries in the parade were beautifully restored classic cars, many from the Fifties and Sixties. Carol leaned forward and yelled to Max "You should have driven your car in the parade!"

Max shook her head. "I don't think we need to draw any more attention—"

A rise in the noise from the crowd interrupted her.

One more float came into view pulled by a pickup. A large tarp covered something in the center. In front of the Jacobsen family, the truck stopped and two people in jeans, hoodie sweatshirts, and Halloween masks jumped out of the bed. They climbed on the rack and pulled off the tarp. Gasps erupted from the crowd.

In the center of the rack, a crude scaffold held a dummy swaying from a noose. A hand-lettered sign was fastened to the straw-stuffed shirt.

Lil squinted at the apparition. "What does it say?"

"I can't tell. It's sideways," Max said. Then the breeze swung the dummy around to face them. The sign said 'George Jacobsen.'

The deputy who had talked to them earlier jogged up to the driver's side of the truck, and from the looks of his wild gestures, directed the driver, also disguised by a mask, to get out of the parade and turn onto the next side street. Pronto.

"Let's get out of here," Carol said, as she maneuvered her walker through the maze of lawn chairs. "I'm really sorry how this turned out."

Lil shook her head as she folded up chairs. "It certainly isn't your fault. I just can't believe that people have held a grudge this long."

Annie helped her mother with the walker. "I guess we should have held the reunion somewhere else. I'm sorry, too, that we're getting this kind of reception. I planned to suggest lunch at Nancy's Diner but let's go to our house and order pizza."

Max watched them pack up and thought how isolated she had been from the fallout from the plant closing. She had left after high school for college and then took a job as a botany professor in Colorado. Most of her close friends had left right after high school, too, so when she went home, it was only for a day or two, and she spent that time with family. Later, her parents came to visit her, rather than the reverse, and then they retired to Florida where their mother died eight years ago and their father five years after that.

She put her hand on Carol's arm. "You—Mom—Dad—none of you even hinted about the backlash you were getting."

Carol shrugged. "You know Mom. She didn't want anything to mar your visits and our time together."

"I feel terrible."

Lil joined them. "Me too."

"Don't," Carol said. "Like I said, this has just blown back up lately. Come on, let's go to Annie's and we can talk about it there."

Annie's twins, six-year-old Paige and Garth, begged to ride in Max's car so Bob and Carol rode with Sharon. The twins' blonde heads bounced in the back seat as they interrupted each other in their eagerness to point out local attractions along the way. Their questions about the car proved a welcome distraction from the stresses of the morning and made Max and Lil laugh all the way to their home.

Annie and Dirk lived on the outskirts of town in a classic Victorian, freshly painted a mossy green with ivory and brown trim. The kids raced to the house. Each wanted to be the one to tell their mother about the ride.

Chapter Four

Annie was on the phone when they walked in. She kept her head ducked, the phone to one ear, and a hand covering the other, trying to hear over the twins' excitement. When she hung up, she motioned Carol out in the kitchen. Lil and Max followed.

"Sorry to be so slow," Carol said over her shoulder.

"Not a problem. What is it?" Lil asked Annie.

Annie looked a little annoyed at the entourage but only briefly. "That was Sheriff Burns. They found Donnie in the back seat of Dutch's car, passed out. They arrested him for the murder and have him in jail."

"Oh, no!" Carol said.

Lil's mouth dropped open. "What the hell?"

"That idiot." Max shook her head.

Annie scanned their faces. "Do you think he did it?"

Max scoffed. "Of course not! It would take too much planning for Donnie."

Annie threw her arms around Carol, nearly knocking over her walker. "Oh, Mom, this was such a bad idea. Why didn't I let you talk me out of having this reunion here?"

Carol patted her back and pulled out a kitchen chair to sit down. "It isn't your fault, dear. Donnie always had a knack for being in the wrong place at the wrong time."

"Well, we'll need to get him a lawyer," Max said. "Carol, is Henry Larsen still practicing?"

"No, he retired, but his son Ted took over. I'll call him. Annie, can you bring me a phone and a phone book?"

They sat quietly while Carol talked to the lawyer. After she hung up, she said, "He doesn't do criminal law but recommended someone from Prairie City. He'll make the contact for us."

"That's nice of him," Lil said.

Max waved the praise away. "Dad pumped plenty of money into that firm. They handled all of the company's legal business."

Lil sighed and frowned at her sister. "Whatever. You're certainly in a mood today."

Max's face tightened. "I don't know why. A family friend was murdered, our brother arrested for it, our dad hung in effigy in a public parade, and the whole town seems to be out to get us. Why would that make anyone crabby?"

Lil leaned her chin on her hand and looked out the window.

Carol looked at Annie. "We'd better get some pizza ordered. Shall I find out what the kids want?" She reached for her walker.

"Sit still," Max said. "I'll do it."

After she left, Lil looked at the others with tears in her eyes. "How can she be so heartless? She's such a bitch sometimes."

Carol shook her head. "It's her way of dealing. I'm surprised you two travel together so much."

That brought a little smile. "It gets a little tense at times, but eventually blows over."

Sharon walked in, carrying Annie's youngest.

"What's going on?"

Carol brought her up to date on the events.

When she finished, Sharon asked, "What are we going to do?"

"Hank Larsen's son Ted is getting him an attorney from Prairie City."

Max returned. "They all want pepperoni so that's easy."

Carol held up her hand as her phone rang. She answered, said "Yes," "I see," "Okay," and hung up. "That was Ted Larsen. He said that the fellow he's trying to get hold of is on the golf course. Saturday, of course. So it could take a while to contact him."

Max nodded. "While you guys are taking care of lunch, I'm going to run down to the jail and see if I can visit Donnie—let him know what we're trying to do for him. What time is the tour this afternoon?"

Annie said, "It's supposed to be at 1:00—should I postpone until 1:30?"

Max shook her head. "We'd have to get hold of everyone, and that would take the time we'd gain. I'll be back as soon as I've talked to him. If they won't let me in because it's lunch time, I'll go back later."

After she went out the door, Carol put her hand on Lil's arm. "See? She's not as heartless as she pretends to be."

THE JAIL CONSISTED of four cells at the back of the courthouse. Castleroll was the county seat, even though Prairie City was in the same county and much larger. Maxine made the request to see her brother and filled out a visitor's form.

When a deputy brought Donnie in to the visitor's room, and Max saw his handcuffs and the orange jumpsuit, a terrible sense of defeat washed over her. She had let her parents down. Donnie was basically a self-centered brat who never had to take responsibility for his own mistakes.

Often she wanted nothing more than to shake him until he could see someone else's problems for a change. But he was her only brother, and as the eldest, she had always been expected to look out for the younger ones. The whole family had spoiled him, which was most of the problem. However, she couldn't shake the weight of her own responsibility.

Donnie's eyes were at half-mast, his face sagging and flushed, and he needed a shave. He sighed when he sat down, and she caught the reek of bad breath. She involuntarily turned her head away.

"Max," he said, his voice pleading.

She turned back and looked at him in disgust. "What? What, this time, Donnie? I suppose none of this is your fault?"

He shrugged and hung his head. "I don't 'member. I need a lawyer."

"Can you pay for one?" She wasn't going to let him off easy. "Maybe we need to get someone appointed by the court."

He turned and stared at the grubby institutional green wall. "I guess."

Max sighed. "Never mind. I talked to Hank Larsen's son Ted. He doesn't practice criminal law but recommended someone from Prairie City. What happened after Sharon dropped you off last night?"

Another shrug. "I don't know."

"Think! You obviously went out again, but you didn't have your truck."

He jumped a little at her angry voice and ran his hand through his curly hair. "J. P. and some of the guys came by, I think. They wanted to go out to the lake—had a couple of twelve packs. Don't get them in trouble."

She slammed her hand on the table. "Dammit, Donnie—this isn't high school. You're sixty years old and charged with murder. Who else besides J. P.? We'll need to talk to them and hope one of them was sober enough to remember events."

"Um, we were at Pete Murphy's place. I don't remember who else. I fell asleep in the grass out at the lake."

"You don't remember how you got in Dutch's car?"
"No idea."
"Did you see or talk to Dutch at all last night?"
"Don't think so."

Maxine got up from her chair. "You'd better start thinking, and fast. The lawyer should be here sometime this afternoon and he—or she—will need answers if they're going to do anything for you."

"Um, can you girls post bail if the judge sets it?"

"No, we can't—or won't. Same difference as far as you're concerned. I'll be back later."

She didn't turn to look at him as she went out, because she knew she would have to go back and give him a hug if she did.

By the time she returned to Annie's, they were loading up cars for the afternoon tour. The old Jacobsen Antenna plant stood just a block off Main Street and consisted of a main building where assembly had taken place, a medium-sized warehouse, and a small office building. After the conglomerate closed the plant, it sat empty for ten years.

George Jacobsen bought the property back and the town buzzed with the possibility of a reopening, but nothing ever happened. The warehouse had been sold to a local fertilizer company, the office building was falling down, and the plant continued to sit empty.

While they waited for the caretaker, Annie told the group, "One of the decisions we need to make this weekend is what to do with this building. It's been for sale, and we've had no interest. The City says we need to tear this and the office down if they aren't going to be used."

A pickup pulled in and a young man jumped out. He smiled at them and greeted Carol and Bob. Carol said, "This is Trevor, Cheryl Jasper's grandson. You remember Mother's friend, Cheryl?"

The older generation nodded and greeted Trevor. He walked to a side door on the loading platform and unlocked a padlock that allowed him to lift a bar and open the door.

"How often do you check the building, Trevor?" Sharon asked.

"About once a week,"

They entered a large assembly room. All the machinery had been removed when George sold the plant. Windows along the south let murky light in the cavernous room and revealed broken cardboard boxes, rags, pieces of antennas, and some items that Max didn't really want to identify that were scattered around the greasy cement floor. Offices with large grimy windows overlooking the plant floor lined one end of the area. A stairway in the corner led up to a mezzanine above the offices.

Max eyed a pile of rags and old blankets in the corner. "Has someone been living here?"

Trevor nodded. "A few months ago. That's why I added the bar and the locks on the access doors, with Mrs. Harstad's permission of course."

Lil looked around and wrinkled her nose at the musty odor. "There wasn't a lock before?"

"Yeah, but they kept breaking in. Kids at first, and then I think there's been a couple of homeless people."

"It looks solid," Sharon said, looking around the building. "But what would it be good for?"

Carol shrugged. "That's why we need input from the family."

"Obviously no business has an interest in using it. What about the school, or the city?" Max asked.

Trevor said, "I have no idea."

"It's big enough for some kind of recreation," Ernie started, but was interrupted by a loud clang. "What was that?"

Trevor seemed to turn pale. "Sounded like the bar on the door." He rushed toward the door and tried to open it. He turned back to them with a look of panic. "We can't get out."

"What about the other doors?" Max asked.

"We had the same bars installed on all of the access doors. The overhead doors haven't been opened in years. We can try."

Annie looked toward the bank of windows on the south. "We could break a window if we have to."

Kim looked at her phone. "We do have phone service. We're not going to die here."

Annie's twins had been chasing each other around the big empty room and came back just in time to hear part of Kim's comment. "Die? We're going to die here?" Paige asked. Her tone of voice didn't carry much concern.

Annie glared at Kim. "No, we aren't going to die here. The bar fell down on the door, so we'll either call for help or break a window."

Garth jumped up and down with excitement. "Can I break the window? Puleeze?"

"It's an adventure!" Paige shouted, spinning around.

Max smiled at Trevor. "See? We adults just have the wrong attitude."

"We'll check the other doors first," Annie told Garth. "You kids stay with me."

"Good idea," Carol grabbed Garth's hand. "We don't need any freelancers."

"What's a free lancer?"

"Never mind. Just stay with me."

"Aw, Grandma." He tugged at her hand.

"Lead on, Trevor," Max said.

The group trooped to three other doors with no luck. All were barred. Trevor led them to the big overhead doors that faced the loading dock. Even with several hands trying, they were unable to budge any of them.

Trevor looked at them apologetically. "I'll have to break a window." He considered the older members of the group. "If I can get out, I'll go around and unbar the door."

"Thank goodness," Lil said. "Not a pretty vision of me trying to crawl through a window."

Garth jumped up and down. "I'll break it! I'll break it!" He raced ahead of them to the window side of the room.

"Wait!" Annie called after him. "Let Trevor show you what to do."

Garth paused and looked uncertainly at Trevor, seemingly sure this guy was going to ruin his fun. Trevor motioned him over to a pile of trash in a corner.

"We need to find something here to use so you won't cut your hand."

They rummaged through the pile and Garth came up with a crowbar.

"That'll work." Trevor grabbed a rag out of the pile as well.

He wrapped the boy's hand with the rag and positioned his sunglasses on Garth's face. Annie stood by wringing her hands. "Be careful, Trevor, okay?"

Trevor nodded and picked Garth up under the arms so that he would not be below the section of window he was breaking.

Garth looked up at Trevor and grinned. "Now?"

"Now." Trevor guided Garth's arm with a gentle swing. The first swing was a little too gentle, but they got it on the second try.

Trevor set Garth back on his feet and took the rag to remove the protruding pieces of glass. He stuck his head out the opening, looked down, and turned back to the group.

"It's a bit of a drop but not bad. There's a ledge below the window that I can stand on. Would a couple of you help me get through this feet first?"

Two of the younger men stepped forward. With a lot of grunts and oofs, they finally got Trevor through on his stomach so that he could find the ledge with his feet and still cling to the window edge. The ground was only about five or six feet below the ledge. He let go, landed with a loud grunt, and gingerly got to his feet.

Max stuck her head out the window. "You okay?"

He brushed himself off and looked up at her. "My ankle might be a little sore tonight but I'm fine. I should have you all out in a jiffy." He hobbled toward the nearest corner of the building.

Chapter Five

THAT HE DID. In less than five minutes, they could hear the heavy bar being lifted from the entry door. Trevor held the door open while the rest rushed through. Lil turned her face up to the sun, welcoming its rays even after such a short confinement.

Max joined her. "I don't think that was an accident. Too much has been going on."

Lil said, "Usually you are too hasty to jump to conclusions, but in this case, you may be right. Someone is organized enough to devise that float in the parade this morning and know our schedule for the afternoon. That's pretty scary."

"I'm going to skip the school tour and see what's happening at Barney's. Bob said that's a good place to pick up the local scuttlebutt."

Lil raised an eyebrow. "Care if I join you?"

"Not at all. I'm going to run out to Carol's first and check on Rosie."

Sharon and Carol said they would stop at the jail to see Donnie.

ON THEIR WAY BACK to town, Max had Lil fish a black chiffon scarf out of her glovebox.

"What are you going to do with this?" Lil held it up.

"We need disguises—not much because we haven't been around for so long. If you want the scarf, I have a little golf hat."

Lil considered as Max pulled a yellow fabric hat out of her door pocket. It must be the brightest thing in her wardrobe, Lil thought. "I'll definitely take the scarf," she said. "Where in the world did you get that hat?"

"I won it in a golf tournament."

"You don't play golf."

"I did once about fifteen years ago in a money raiser for the Botany Department scholarship fund. I won that hat."

Lil laughed. "Highest score?"

"Most lost balls."

Lil arranged the scarf over her hair and then wrapped it around her neck.

Sort of an Audrey Hepburn look, Max thought. She crammed the yellow hat over her own gray bob.

Max surveyed Barney's as they entered. A typical small-town bar just at the edge of scruffy and dingy. Music played under the Saturday afternoon voices, but Max couldn't identify it. She and Lil took seats at the end of the bar. Her hat garnered several amused looks, but no one indicated recognition or even much interest in their presence. She ordered a Coors Lite and Lil asked for a glass of white wine.

Max raised her eyebrows. "*Any* white wine?"

"It doesn't look like a place you could be picky."

"True."

They sipped their drinks in silence, not being antisocial but trying to eavesdrop on other conversations. Most seemed to be a discussion of sports or the farm outlook. Lil tilted her head toward a group behind her in a booth, and gave Max a look. They both concentrated on the men's voices.

"Cec Ridley ain't gonna give up until he gets some money out of them Jacobsens," one said.

Another gave a loud laugh. "He's dreamin'."

"They don't want publicity, that's for sure. Why d'ya think Dutch is dead?"

"I heard they got Donnie Jacobsen for it."

"Huh. There's plenty of others who weren't happy with Dutch."

"My wife says Junie Coonley worried about what he was gonna put in his book about her."

"I bet she did. Gotta go. See you guys later."

Chairs scraped, goodbyes were exchanged, and doors slammed.

"Well," Max said in a low voice. "Might be something there. Junie Coonley? Buzz Coonley's little sister?"

"Not so little any more." The bartender wiped the bar in front of them and waggled his eyebrows.

Both women jumped at the sound of his voice.

"Sorry." Now he winked at them. "Shouldn't have been eavesdropping."

Max thought he referred to them. "We weren't. I should say, we didn't mean to."

"I meant me," he said. "Can I get you refills?"

Lil stood up and laid a five on the bar. "No, thanks. We need to be going."

Max laid a hand on Lil's arm. "Wait a minute." She turned to the bartender. "Do you know if Pete Murphy still lives in town?"

"Pete Murphy lives in a trailer out by the lake."

"Okay, thanks." She laid a couple of bills on the bar and led the way back into the sunshine.

ONCE OUTSIDE, Lil said, "Pete Murphy? Donnie's old friend?"

"That's who he was with last night after Sharon dropped him at the motel. Pete and J.P. Prentiss is all he can remember, and he's not real sure about that. But he said they were drinking out at the lake and he fell asleep in the grass. We need to talk to Pete and J.P. — I'm pretty sure J.P's still around too."

"Maybe they'll be at the picnic tomorrow?"

"Maybe. Otherwise we can run out to the lake after the picnic and see if we can find Pete."

BY THE TIME they returned to Annie's house, the rest of the family had as well.

"Did you see Donnie?" Lil asked Carol and Sharon.

"Yes," Carol said. "He's still feeling sorry for himself, but his lawyer is supposed to come by about 6:00. He asked us again about bail. We could—"

Max shook her head. "I know it's late in the game, but we've got to stop enabling him. We'll look at bail tomorrow after he's seen the lawyer. Maybe more information will come out by then on who really did kill Dutch."

Max and Lil were about to share what they had overheard at the bar when the doorbell rang.

Paige raced to the door, shouting, "I'll get it!" She opened the door and yelled "Whoa!"

"Who is it?" Annie called.

"The cops!" Paige entered the kitchen waving her hands like she was leading a parade. The sheriff, a man of medium height, a slight belly, and round face topped by wispy tufts of blond hair, followed.

He smiled. "That's quite a reception."

Annie wiped her hands on a towel and greeted him. "Sheriff, I'm sorry. I just assumed it was another family member." She gestured to the group in the kitchen. "We're having a family reunion this weekend."

"So I gathered, and I'm sorry to interrupt, but I need to talk to—" he looked around, "—the adults, if I may?"

"Sure," Annie said. She looked around the room and spotted Kim and Ernie's daughter. "Chelsea, would you take the kids in and put a video on for them? Paige and Garth will show you where they are."

Chelsea frowned, but nodded and herded the young ones toward the living room.

Max assumed she was not happy about missing out on the murder talk, or whatever the sheriff was there for.

Sharon pulled out a chair at the table. "Sit, please, Sheriff. Would you like some coffee?"

"That would be great." He laid his hat on the table. As if by plan, Max, Lil, Carol, and Sharon took other chairs at the table and the others perched on the bar stools or leaned against the cabinets. Annie brought the sheriff a mug of coffee along with a spoon, sugar, and creamer. She sat in the last chair at the table.

There was a lot of shifting and throat-clearing while the sheriff added sweetener to his coffee and stirred. He aligned his spoon along side his mug and looked around the room.

"For those of you who don't know me, I'm Sheriff John Burns. It sounds to me like you've had more excitement at this reunion than you planned?"

Several nodded, and Ernie blurted, "What about Donnie?"

"I'll get to that in a minute. First, Trevor Jasper called me. You folks had a little trouble at the old plant?"

Annie said, "It might have been an accident—"

The sheriff shook his head. "Trevor didn't think so. He said that bar has to be lifted and put in place. Now, that smells like more of a prank than an attempt to actually harm anyone. Then my deputy, Specs Johnson, told me about the float in the parade this morning. And all that after we find your brother asleep in a murder victim's car. So, who wants to tell me what's going on?"

Annie started to speak, but Max held up her hand. "To sum it up, Sheriff, we don't know. Obviously there're still bad feelings about the closing of our father's business, but for heaven's sake—that was forty years ago. Carol is the only one who still lived here at the time, and she wasn't involved in the business. I'm sure you know better than us whether this is a widespread vendetta or a few disgruntled souls."

He raised his eyebrows and leaned back to look at her. "Disgruntled? Disgruntled may have locked you in the plant or hung your father in effigy, but disgruntled doesn't commit murder."

"Are you sure they're connected?" Lil asked.

"We're not sure of anything. If your brother is responsible for Dutch Schneider's murder, there could very well be a connection."

"Our brother has been known to be lazy, irresponsible, and immature, but I guarantee you he's not a murderer," Carol said.

"Then why isn't the family willing to post bail?"

Max folded her hands and fixed the sheriff with an icy stare. "Our brother has an alcohol problem. If he didn't, he would know where he spent last night and be able to provide an alibi. We have 'bailed him out' a number of times when he gets in financial trouble, and this time we're trying to impress on him that he needs to start taking responsibility for himself. I have a question for you. We have heard rumors that there were several others in town who won't miss Dutch Schneider. Do you know anything about that?"

He looked skeptical. "Can you give me names?"

She faltered and examined her fingernails. "Well, no."

"Julie Coonley!" Lil blurted.

The eyebrows went up again. "Junie?"

Lil nodded. "That's it. Junie. You know her?"

"She's the town mayor," Carol said quietly.

"Aha!" Lil slapped the table. "Did she have a beef with Dutch?"

Burns shook his head. "Really can't say."

"Can't or won't?" Max asked.

"Max!" Carol put her hand on her sister's shoulder and gave her a stern look.

Max sighed and rolled her eyes but said no more.

Lil snapped her fingers. "Sheriff, we also heard that Cecil Ridley thinks we owe him money. He moved the rope that Annie put up this morning to save our parade seats, even though lots of others had saved spots with lawn chairs. Have you talked to him?"

He sighed. "I hardly think that's in the same category with these other—um—actions. Getting back to the incident at the plant—have there been any threats toward your family?"

Max said, "Our father was hung in effigy. You don't consider that a threat?"

The sheriff ignored her.

"Carol or Annie would have to answer that. None of the rest of us maintain much contact with the community any more, right?" Lil looked around at the rest. No one spoke.

"I've never heard of any threats," Carol said. "It's always just been a few dirty looks or veiled comments."

Annie nodded agreement.

"Tell me where you all were last night and early this morning. Normally, I would interview you individually, but we don't have the manpower or time this weekend with a murder and the Festival going on."

"That's simple, Sheriff. We were all out at Carol and Bob's last night for a potluck supper. Most people left between nine and ten," Max said.

"Donnie Jacobsen was there?"

"Most definitely," Sharon said. "We took him back to his motel about 10:00 and left his truck at the farm. He was in no shape to go anywhere else."

"But apparently he did," Sheriff Burns said. "How about the rest of you this morning?"

"We were all at the parade," Max said. "Then back here for pizza, and then the tour of the plant. I went down to visit Donnie while they were having pizza."

"Okay." He got up and set his coffee mug on the counter. "Thank you for your time."

Lil got up and blocked the sheriff's way to the door. "What about Donnie? We heard Dutch was killed with a piece of antenna. Were Donnie's fingerprints on it?"

Sheriff Burns hesitated and finally said, "It had been wiped clean."

"That's very important. Like Sharon said, we didn't think he was in any shape to go anywhere, but apparently some of his buddies came by and picked him up. But no way could he have thought far enough ahead to wipe his fingerprints off a murder weapon."

Burns shrugged. "It's an open investigation." He took out a notepad. "Do you know the names of the friends who picked him up?"

Carol gave him the names.

He wrote them down. "All right. Remember, we are still checking all leads."

"That's all we ask," Lil said. She walked the sheriff to the door and closed it behind him.

Bob looked at Max and Lil. "Where did you ladies pick up this info about our esteemed mayor?"

Lil looked blank a moment. "Oh! You mean Julie—er Junie—Coonley? We stopped at Barney's after we checked on Rosie. A bunch of guys in a booth behind us were not quiet about their suspicions. They talked about that Cecil, too."

"What did they say about Donnie? Anything?"

"They kind of brushed that off. Mentioned that Cecil wanted a big payoff from us—made it sound like blackmail, maybe" Max said. "Then someone said he heard Junie was afraid Dutch had something about her in his book."

Bob brushed his thinning hair back. "There've been rumors that she and Dutch were having an affair."

"Why would he have written about that? Was he planning to leave town and didn't care what people thought?"

Bob shrugged. "Don't know."

"There's a lot we don't know if we're going to help Donnie," Max said. "Like where are these documents about the sales of Jacobsen Antenna that he supposedly had, and where's the manuscript for his book?"

Sharon laughed. "What, Max—are you a detective now?"

"She's right," Lil said. "We don't know anything about this attorney Ted Larsen recommended, and I doubt if the sheriff's department has much experience in investigating murders."

Dirk said, "The only ones I can remember in the last ten years were either bar fights or domestic issues. Pretty cut and dried."

"It won't hurt to do a little investigating on our own," Max said. "Annie? Supper is at 5:30?"

"Yes, at the VFW. You remember where that is?"

"I do if it hasn't moved." Max looked at Lil. "I need to change clothes. You?"

"Definitely," Lil said getting up. "I have three outfits I haven't worn yet."

Carol said, "We'll be along soon, too."

MAX HAD CHANGED and was waiting for the others on the patio, giving Rosie the attention she demanded, when her cell phone rang.

"Max?" A woman's voice, harsh and accusing.

"Yes. Who is this?"

"It's Janet, of course. What's going on with Donnie?"

Max took a deep breath. Donnie's wife. Not an easy woman to deal with in the best of circumstances, and this situation fell far short of that. Rosie sensed the tension, got up from her sprawl in the shade, and put her head in Max's lap. Max tried to explain as succinctly as possible what had occurred.

"What are you doing about it? Did you get him a lawyer?"

"Yes, we did, Janet, but it's the weekend and I don't know if he has seen Donnie yet. He's from Prairie City. Are you coming over?" Donnie and Janet lived in Milwaukee.

"Well, no, of course not. I'm very busy. There should be plenty of you there to get this taken care of."

Somehow it didn't feel like a vote of confidence.

"I'm sorry to hear that. I imagine Donnie would appreciate your support."

"I would appreciate his support and I never seem to get it."

"I understand, but that's not the issue right now, is it?"

"Just keep me informed." She was gone.

Max sat staring at the phone as Bob helped Carol out the door. Carol read the anger on her sister's face.

"Who was that?"

"Our favorite sister-in-law."

"Janet? Must be since she's also your only sister-in-law. She what—wants to pay for Donnie's lawyer? Is putting up bail? Is rushing right over to be by her husband's side?"

Max gave a humorless laugh. "We must not be talking about the same person."

Bob rubbed his hands together. "Should I go punch her in the face?"

That broke Max's funk. She let loose a guffaw. "Please do. I'll hold her for you."

"What's so funny?" Lil stepped out in denim leggings and a white blouse edged in lace that she had picked up in Mexico.

Max related Janet's call. Lil just shook her head. "She is never going to change. So are we ready to go?"

Chapter Six

THE VFW WAS IN THE BASEMENT of the old five-and-dime and reached by an outside stairway descending from the sidewalk. Even though smoking hadn't been allowed for years, the gray, dry smell still seemed to emanate from the walls. The bartender directed Max and Lil to a room at the back.

Annie greeted them. "Sorry it's not fancy."

Lil patted her on the arm. "We just appreciate all the work you've done to organize this weekend. I don't imagine there're many choices in town."

Annie smiled. "Thank you. No, there aren't, but the food is really good here."

The long tables were covered with white paper. A couple of small flag arrangements provided the only decoration. Places were set with stainless flatware—probably obtained with Betty Crocker coupons, Max thought—and plain paper napkins.

Soon after they got themselves seated, an older woman began serving salads. She was not tall but large-busted with an imposing stomach under a Vikings tee shirt. Her mouse-gray hair was pinned back from a round face. She looked familiar, but Max couldn't place her.

The salads consisted of crunchy romaine and other greens, fresh red tomatoes, feta cheese, and a light oil and herb dressing. After the waitress passed, Max picked up her fork and leaned over to Carol. "Who is that?"

Carol turned around to look and said, "Bonnie Webb — was Bonnie Johnson." She grinned and got the reaction she expected.

"Bonnie *Johnson*? You're kidding me." Max watched the woman efficiently place the salads and leave the room. Lil looked at her with raised eyebrows.

"I never would have guessed," Max said. Bonnie Johnson had been in her class, a cheerleader, and a Debbie Reynolds look-alike. She had been petite and bouncy and loved by everyone in the class, although many of the girls, including Max, were secretly jealous of Bonnie's looks and personality. Max always felt like an Amazon next to Bonnie.

"She never left town — like me —" Carol said, "and married Junior Webb, raised four kids — nice kids too. Junior lost his job when the plant closed and about a year later, got on at the meat packing plant in Prairie City. He retired at 65 and died of a heart attack six months later. She's been working here ever since."

"Oh my," Max said. "What a sad story."

"Well, it ended sadly, but they always seemed happy."

When Bonnie returned to pick up the salad bowls, Max said "Bonnie?"

Bonnie's smile became more intense. "Maxine? That is you, isn't it?"

"Yes, it is. It's good to see you." Max slid her chair out so that she could face Bonnie without craning her neck.

Bonnie juggled the bowls she was holding and held out her right hand. "Where do you live now?"

"Colorado."

"You never come back for the class reunions. I always hoped you would."

Max was surprised. She and Bonnie had never been close friends.

"Several times I was tied down teaching summer school. And I was always a little worried about my reception after the plant closed."

Bonnie waved a hand and laughed—still the same infectious bubbling laugh. "That didn't have anything to do with you, did it? You really should join us. We'll have another one in two years. Do we have your address?"

"Thank you. Maybe I'll try to make the next one. I still get the mailings so you must have the correct address."

"Good. I need to get back to work, but will I see you at the picnic tomorrow?"

"That's the plan. Good to see you." As Bonnie moved down the table, Max felt lighter than she had since they arrived. If Bonnie didn't hold a grudge, maybe it was only a vocal few.

The salad had been a pleasant surprise to Max who had expected a wedge of iceberg swimming in bottled dressing. The entree included perfectly grilled chicken breasts, slices of rare roast beef, garlic mashed potatoes, and tender early sweet corn.

"I've died and gone to heaven," Max said. "I haven't had corn this good in decades."

Lil agreed. "The whole meal is excellent."

Annie smiled, as she grabbed a fork away from her youngest, who had been banging it on the table. "I'm glad you like it. Although a disclaimer--the corn's from Missouri. It isn't ready around here yet. The place isn't fancy, but the cook is a hometown boy who returned from an upscale restaurant in Chicago to take care of his mother. You wouldn't know them—they moved here after you left."

After the meal, Carol and Bob invited the group back to their house, but they decided instead to remain around the table visiting for a while. After the stressful day, they wanted an early night. Several ordered drinks.

Max offered a toast to Annie. "Thank you again for organizing this. In spite of the problems—out of your control—it was a great idea."

"Hear! Hear!" the others chorused.

"Thank you, Aunt Max. I just wish Uncle Donnie was here with us."

Sharon shook her head. "Poor Donnie—spending the weekend in jail."

"While I don't believe for a minute that he is guilty of this charge, he's gotten away with so much in his lifetime. It isn't going to hurt him." Max fixed Sharon with a firm stare, leaving no doubt where she stood.

Lil jumped in to defuse things. "Annie, don't get me wrong. This meal has been great. But aren't there any other venues in town for gatherings like this, or wedding receptions, for example?"

Annie shook her head. "Small receptions are sometimes held in the church basements, but if the couple wants a dance and a more elaborate meal, they go out of town."

"That's too bad." Lil turned to Carol. "You were asking what to do with the plant building. Is there any possibility of turning it into some kind of community center that could be used for meetings, receptions, that kind of thing?"

"It would be expensive," Bob said. "The heating would need to be updated, air conditioning installed, not to mention cosmetic upgrades."

"And the window fixed." Annie grinned.

"There is memorial money that we haven't done anything with," Carol said. "It might be worth exploring."

Lil twisted her napkin into a spiral. "Maybe a peace offering to soothe these old grudges."

Max wasn't so sure. "The people who are still angry would see it as a bribe."

"You're always so negative, Max." Lil threw her napkin on the table.

"There aren't as many as you think, Aunt Max," Annie said.

Max sighed. "I admit, I was encouraged after talking to Bonnie, but then I keep seeing that scaffold."

She got up to visit the restroom in the front of the club. The tables in the barroom had filled up and the noise was deafening. On her way back, someone grabbed her sleeve.

Startled, she looked down at an older woman sitting at one of the tables. Well, maybe not older than her. Thin with black hair but enough facial wrinkles to give away the dye job.

"Maxine Jacobsen? Tess—Tess Browning. Remember me?"

"Oh my Lord, Tess! I haven't seen you in eons!"

Tess pulled her down toward the next chair. "Can you sit a minute?"

"Um, sure. How are you?"

"Fine—I'm Tess Robinson now, though. And you?"

"Berra is my last name but I've been divorced for years. No kids and it was amicable."

Tess smiled and put her hand on Max's. "I don't think I've seen you since about three years after we graduated."

Max laughed and nodded. "Patsy's wedding. She never forgave us for the grass and straw we filled the back seat of her car with."

Tess literally hooted. They began to reminisce about trick-or-treating as kids and asking for money instead of treats, piling seven or eight friends in one car to go to basketball games, and staying up all night to finish English papers on *Paradise Lost*.

"Remember when we broke into the school and made that stupid recording on the music department's tape recorder? Changed our voices?"

"Not well enough," Max said. "Mr. Berg recognized us the next time he tried to record the boy's chorus contest piece."

Tess put her hand on her chest, gasping for air. "Oh my! I haven't laughed so hard since I don't know when. So your whole family's in town?"

"Most of us. Some people aren't too happy about it." She told Tess about the incident at the plant and parade float.

"You're kidding! I didn't get to the parade because my granddaughter had a softball tournament in Prairie City. Who would do such a thing?"

Max shrugged. "I suppose you heard about Donnie being arrested for Dutch Schneider's murder?"

"No! I mean, I heard about Dutch, but we just got back to town a couple of hours ago. Why Donnie?"

"They found him passed out this morning in Dutch's car. And Dutch was stabbed with part of an old TV antenna, so I suppose that added to it."

"We wondered what had happened to you!" Carol came up behind Max's chair. "Hi Tess, how are you?"

"Great!" Tess said. "Max just told me about what a day you guys have had."

Carol nodded. "Not the kind of reunion we envisioned. I'll leave you two to catch up. Max, most of us are going to be leaving soon. Lil can ride with us if you want to stay longer."

"Fine—or she can join us if she wants."

"I'll tell her."

After Carol left, Max leaned in toward Tess, confident that the loud voices and music would cover her questions.

"Do you know the mayor?"

"Junie? She's right up there at the bar—the blonde in the red tee."

Max looked over and was surprised to see a slim woman who appeared to be in her late thirties or early forties, perched on a stool between two men. She threw back her head in laughter, her shoulder-length hair whipped with the motion of her head, and then she turned to the man on her left and gave him a sly look. She batted him on the shoulder, but Max couldn't hear what was being said.

"So we overheard that she was having an affair with Dutch, but she looks like she's forty years younger than he was. Did you ever hear anything like that?"

Tess smiled. "That was the rumor, and I think there was something to it. And she isn't *that* much younger."

"She doesn't look like she's in mourning or anything."

"No, she doesn't. That's her husband on the right side."

Max shook her head. "This is crazy. We heard that she was worried that Dutch was going to include her in his memoirs. We also heard that some guy — Cecil somebody — was mad at Dutch for not disclosing documents that he claims Dutch has about the sale of my dad's plant."

Tess nodded. "Those are all possible. Dutch had made a lot of enemies by the time he sold the paper."

"What about this new guy? Comar?"

"Charlie Gomar. He wrote an editorial accusing Dutch of covering up stuff."

Lil pulled out a chair on the other side of Tess. "It looks like you two are plotting something."

"The opposite," Max said. "Trying to uncover a plot."

Tess greeted Lil and asked about her family. Lil had been two years behind Max and Tess's class.

"So," Lil said, "have you got this thing solved?"

"All we have is rumors," Max said. "We need to find some concrete evidence. I'd like to see a copy of this memoir."

Tess grinned. "Dutch still lived in that upstairs apartment in Lareen Mantle's house."

"Good Lord! Is she still alive?" Lil said.

"Heavens, no. She died ten or fifteen years ago. No one's lived in the downstairs apartment since. We always thought Dutch would buy the house or at least move downstairs, he didn't. He must pay enough rent that Lareen's grandchildren never bothered to rent the bottom. What I'm saying is, now the house is empty."

Max leaned back in her chair. "Are you suggesting what I think you're suggesting?"

Tess shrugged. "The Dastardly Duo rides again."

"Trio," Lil said. "The Terrible Trio. You guys would never take me along in the old days."

"Because you were always a tattletale. So if you don't tell the sheriff, you can go," Max said.

"Goody," Lil said with a smile. "After only sixty years, you've forgiven me."

Chapter Seven

TESS OFFERED TO DRIVE. Her dark compact SUV would be much less noticeable on the streets than Max's Studebaker. She drove to an older neighborhood on the west side of town and down a road that ended in a dead end. Dutch's apartment was in a two-story, once-white house. A roof supported with wrought iron posts sheltered a small front porch in an ell formed by two wings of the house. There were no lights on anywhere.

As Tess cruised by slowly, Max could see an outside stairway partially hidden behind one of the wings. A gravel driveway ran along the side and curved behind the house. All of these older homes sat on large lots with tall trees and shrubs.

"Perfect," Max breathed. "We can get in and out with no one the wiser."

Lil leaned forward from the back seat. "You guys are really going to do this?"

Max rolled her eyes. "What did you think we were going to do? Tess, do you have a flashlight?"

"Check the glove box."

"The door's probably locked," Lil said.

"Probably." Tess held up a credit card. "And if this doesn't work we won't get in. But we'll give it a try. Coming?" She got out of the car.

Max hurried around the front to join her and Lil crept behind.

"This isn't a good—" Lil started, but Max turned around to shush her.

"You wanted to come so no complaining. You're taking your purse?"

"I'm not leaving it in the car."

Max rolled her eyes again, an ineffective gesture in the dark. "Right. Someone might break in. C'mon—let's get this done."

The wooden stairway, devoid of paint, had boards so weathered they did not look like they would hold anyone.

"We'll be lucky if we don't all break a leg," Lil whispered.

Tess shook her head and led up the stairs. "Can't be that bad. Dutch was *not* a small man, and he used them until yesterday."

The steps protested, sometimes loudly, but held. Each time a step creaked or snapped, they stopped and looked around, but all else was quiet. Fortunately the steps ended in an oversized landing at the top, so they could all gather around the door under an extended roof. A plastic lawn chair stood in one corner of the porch. Next to the door was a high window.

Max tried to peer in. "I can't see anything," she whispered.

Tess tried the door first, but it was locked. She maneuvered her credit card between the jamb and the door, while Max held the light and Lil looked around as if expecting ghouls to jump out of the darkness.

"Rats!" Tess stood back, but kept the light on the door. "No luck."

Max took the light from her and shone it on the window. There was no screen and the paint was badly chipped. "This window doesn't even have a latch." She handed Tess back the light and pushed up gently on the bottom sash. Nothing happened.

Tess gave the light to Lil. "Let me help." They both pushed, careful not to separate the disintegrating sash from the glass.

"It moved! We need something to get underneath it," Max said. She glanced back at Lil. "What do you have in that purse that would fit in this little gap so we can pry it up?"

Lil handed her the flashlight and started digging in a bag the size of most carry-ons. A tiny screwdriver was tried and rejected; nail clippers not even tried; and a table knife was also unsuccessful.

"I won't even ask why you have a table knife in your purse," Max said.

"I don't like plastic. What about this?" She pulled an ice scraper out of the bottom.

Tess grabbed it. "That should do the trick." She wedged the scraper under the bottom sash and gently pried. The window edged up, screeching in protest. The noise caused them to glance around, looking for lights coming on or a stray jogger taking interest, but there was nothing. Tess got her fingers under the window and raised it as far as it would go.

"Now what?" Lil asked.

Max pulled the plastic lawn chair over. "I'm going in and then I'll unlock the door."

"Are you sure?" Tess asked. "Lil is younger."

"Hell, we're all over seventy. What difference does it make?" Max hefted herself onto the chair seat and stuck one leg through the window. "There's a counter there—must be the kitchen." She paused and pulled the leg back, opting to go through the window head and arms first. Halfway in, her butt and legs still hanging outside, she stopped again.

Tess started to laugh, covering her mouth to keep the noise down and Lil soon joined in.

Max grumbled, "Well, don't just stand there. Help me back out. This isn't going to work." Tess grabbed her around the waist and tugged. She slowly emerged and stood on the chair again.

"You have to go feet first so you can sit on the counter and then get down. Want me to do it?" Tess swatted a mosquito away from her face.

"I can do it, but you two will have to hold me up so I can get my other leg in." She put her right leg in and held her arms out, teetering precariously until Tess and Lil each grabbed an arm. Tess helped swing the left leg up into the window amidst grunts and groans from all three.

"Yeow!" Max yelped, as they tried to slide her over the rough window jamb. The sound of fabric ripping brought another groan from Max. "My favorite linen pants!"

She grabbed the inside of the window frame to pull herself in. Another ouch as she hit her head on the window.

"At least it won't hurt your hairdo," Lil said.

"Very funny."

Finally she could sit up on the counter and let herself down to the floor. In the process, something rolled off the counter and crashed.

"Give me the light." She held her hand out the window. Tess put it in her hand and Max turned to see where she had landed.

"Get the door open first," Tess hissed. "We've been lucky so far, but I don't want to stand out here longer than necessary."

Max bustled around and got the door unlocked. As Lil closed it quietly behind them, Max shone the light around the apartment. A jar of jam lay broken on the kitchen floor. The living room, just off the kitchen, held one oversized recliner, a broken-looking sofa, a huge flat-screen TV, and a large desk in one corner.

"Dutch wasn't much of a decorator." Lil said.

Max headed for the corner. "We need to check the desk first." A laptop computer sat closed on the desk top and a printer in the back corner. Max opened the laptop and the screen sprang to life.

"Good." Tess rubbed her hands together. "He didn't even log out."

Lil looked around while Max brought up the documents file. "I can't believe the sheriff hasn't been here and taken his records."

Max scrolled through the file names. "I don't see anything that looks like a manuscript, unless he's given it a fake name."

Tess went in the bedroom, closed the drapes and turned on a small table lamp. She opened the closet and started pulling boxes off the shelf. "Lil, come in and help me with this stuff."

Max peeked around the corner of the doorway. Tess had five or six boxes on the bed and searched through each. Lil started on one at the other end of the row.

Max went back to the computer screen. The file names looked mostly like news articles: council election, water plant, homecoming court, and so on. She considered that these might be topics in his manuscript and opened one of the council files. It read like a news story—dry statements about votes, budgets and appointments. She tried another one. Same thing. As she scrolled on, a file title caught her eye: Jacobsen plant.doc.

Maybe this was something. But she opened it to find nothing—a blank Word doc. She closed it and checked the date on the file. It was dated ten years earlier. Why would someone delete the content of the file instead of the whole file? Or maybe Dutch created a file but never wrote anything.

Tess and Lil came out of the bedroom. "Nothing remotely close," Tess said. "Check registers, photos, paperback books."

"One box has nothing but old ties, all rolled up. Most of them wrinkled and grease-spotted."

Max closed the laptop and stood up from the desk. She took the flashlight from Lil and played the beam around the living room again. The couch was one of the saddest pieces of furniture that she had ever seen. The lumpy cushions cantered at odd angles, and the back appeared to be frameless in spots. She walked over and pulled up an end cushion. A box that would hold a ream of printer paper was shoved down in a corner, distorting the cushions.

"Lookee here, ladies." She pulled the box out and set it on a wobbly side table. The aqua ceramic table lamp teetered and crashed to the floor.

Lil rushed to pick it up. "Max! Take it easy."

Max eyed the lamp. "Looks like no loss to me." She pulled the lid off the box and used the flashlight to examine the top piece of paper.

"I think this is it."

A crash from the kitchen made them freeze. Scrambling sounds followed. Max picked up the box and crept toward the door, keeping the light ahead of her. If someone was there—and what else could it be?—she could blind them temporarily with the light while the others got away.

Tess and Lil followed close behind. At first, they couldn't see anyone. Max aimed the light toward a scratching sound near the floor.

Max let out a deep breath. "There's the culprit, girls." A grey squirrel nibbled the spilled jam until the light hit him. He froze a moment and then scurried toward the back of the kitchen.

Lil screeched and dashed for the outside door. Tess followed. "Right behind you, sister."

Carrying the box, Max kept the light on the squirrel and backed out the door.

"Hold this." She thrust the box toward Tess, pulled the sash most of the way down on the window, and put the chair back. "Let's get out of here."

"What about the door lock?" Tess asked.

Max shook her head. "Nobody's going to know whether Dutch locked his door or not." She led the way down the stairs.

"You can't leave that squirrel in there," Lil hissed.

"I just did. He'll find his way back to the window, but by the time he's done rampaging around in there, he'll cover our tracks." They retraced their steps to the car, watching for any signs of observers. "It's perfect. Dutch left the window cracked for air and the squirrel got in. Knocked the jam off the counter, broke the lamp, who knows what else?"

Tess started her car, but sat there a minute. "I don't know, Max. If we find any clues in that manuscript, how are you going to explain to the sheriff how you got it?"

Max stared out the window, thinking, and then looked back at Tess. "We can go through it tonight, and I'll put it back early in the morning, before he has a chance to search."

"That won't explain how you know anything you find out," Lil said.

Max sighed. "Let's go back to Carol's and see what we've got. We can talk about the consequences if we find anything. Drop me back at the VFW so I can pick up my car. Are you going home, Tess, or are you going to join us?"

"I didn't go through all of this to just go home and go to bed."

Chapter Eight

Lil opted to ride with Tess. She was angry with Max over the incident which made Max wonder why she went along in the first place. She wanted to be a part of everything, but she was such a chicken. Chickens reminded her of squirrels, and she chuckled to herself about their unexpected accomplice in the break in, as she started the Studebaker and pulled out behind Tess.

There had to be a clue in the manuscript. She glanced at the box in the passenger seat to reassure herself that it was still there. She drove much slower than Tess on the gravel road to avoid getting her car any dustier than necessary. She got to the farm, retrieved the box, and locked her car. By the time she got in the house, Carol looked at her in disbelief, and Bob gave her an icy stare. Rosie, on the other hand, ran up to her and licked her hand.

"Couldn't wait to spill the beans, could you?" Max said to Lil.

"It was stupid."

"Then you shouldn't have gone."

"I didn't think you'd really do it."

Bob shook his head. "It was stupid. What were you—any of you—thinking?"

Max was surprised and hurt. In the forty-some years that Bob and Carol had been married, he had never criticized or said a cross word to her. They had always gotten along well, and shared a similar sense of humor and political views. This was too much. Didn't they realize Donnie's freedom was at stake?

"I was *thinking* that *some*one had to do *some*thing. Donnie's in jail. We all know he's not guilty, but I'm not convinced your sheriff is sharp enough to look beyond the bird in the hand."

Carol put her hand on Max's arm. "Maxine, please remember that we have to live here. You can take off and not face any of the gossip." Her voice was gentle and pleading. Always the peacemaker.

Max shook her hand off. "Maybe I should go stay in the motel. It doesn't sound like I'm welcome here any more."

"Max," Carol pleaded. "Don't be like that. We all want to help Donnie. Let's see what you found and we can talk about the repercussions later. C'mon—sit down. I've made some coffee."

Max reluctantly put the box on the table and pulled out a chair. She refrained for the time being from glaring at Lil. "All of the suspects we have heard mentioned—Junie Coonley, Cecil Ridley, Charlie Gomar—are somehow connected to this manuscript. Maybe Sheriff Burns would eventually get to it, but he's obviously shorthanded. Okay, it was dumb to break in there. But we have it now. If we divide it up, we can scan it and look for names. Then I'll take it back."

Tess grinned. "What if the squirrel's still in there?"

"Squirrel?" Bob asked.

"A squirrel got in," Lil said. "We left the window open."

"You went in through a *window*?"

"Just Max did," Tess said. "She unlocked the door for us."

"Lord." Bob smoothed his hair and leaned back in his chair. "I wish I had seen that." He tried to keep a straight face but started to laugh. Guffaws exploded from deep in his chest until he gasped for breath.

Finally he took a deep breath and wiped his eyes. "That doesn't make it any less dumb. All right, let's see what's in that box." He kept shaking his head. "Carol used to tell me stories about you and Tess when you were young, and I thought they were exaggerated. Now I can see they were not. She probably toned them down."

Max glanced at Tess, shrugged, and opened the paper box. She lifted out a stack of paper. After looking at the last page, she said, "There's 150 pages here. So if we each take thirty and skim them looking for names, maybe we can find something." She divided them up, handing each of the others a stack.

For the next hour, the only sound was the shuffling of pages, with an occasional scrape of a chair for a coffee refill. Carol had put a package of sticky flags in the center of the table to mark pages they thought might be pertinent. She also added a plate of oatmeal cookies with white chocolate chunks and macadamia nuts for sustenance.

The first time Lil reached for one of the flags, she said, "I might have something here."

Max frowned at her. "Just mark it and when we're all done, we'll go through everything we find."

Lil's face fell, but she didn't say anything and went back to her search. Bob uttered a little 'oh-ho' once as he reached for a flag. Tess said 'hmmm' or 'wow' several times before marking something. Even Max had a couple of eyebrow raises. But they all resisted elaborating until they were finished.

"Okay, I was going to return this early in the morning, but I should take it back before we go over these. Let's make copies of the marked pages and then I'll run it into town," Max said.

Carol and Max took the stacks into the home office. Max used the stickies to find each pertinent page, removed the flag, and handed the page to Carol who made a copy.

Max stacked the pages in order and replaced them in the box. "Well, I'd better get this back to Dutch's apartment."

Carol laid her hand on Bob's arm. "Honey, you should go with her."

Seeing the look of panic on Bob's face, Max objected. "Absolutely not. You'll have enough embarrassment if I get caught, but at least you'll have 'plausible deniability,' as the politicians say."

Tess got up. "I'll go. In for a penny, in for a pound."

They took Tess' car again and soon were back behind the house with Dutch's apartment. Max groaned a little as she got out of the car—this escapade was taking a toll on her knees. And she still had to climb the stairs.

She huffed up the steps behind Tess. "I'm sure glad we left the door unlocked. I couldn't do the window again."

Tess opened the door and aimed her flashlight inside. "I don't see the squirrel, but he made a heck of a mess."

Max followed her in, and they headed for the living room. Tess held the light while Max lifted the couch cushion and shoved the box back under it. They had just reached the kitchen when a dull thud came from the bedroom.

"The squirrel?" Tess whispered.

Footsteps sounded and a door closed. "No. Let's get out of here."

They hurried down the steps trying to avoid a twisted ankle at the same time. They didn't worry about slamming the car doors or seat belts, and Tess soon had them racing away from the cul de sac.

Tess got her breath and said, "Jessica Fletcher wouldn't have run away."

"That's why we're not on TV."

"Who do you think was in there? Couldn't have been anyone who was supposed to be—like the sheriff, for instance."

"The sheriff wouldn't be there in the dark. My first guess would be the murderer, but it could be anyone who thinks that manuscript would give him—or her—trouble. Or maybe they were looking for something else."

Tess shrugged. "You're right. It's wide open. It may not even be connected to his murder."

It was almost midnight by the time they returned. Bob dozed in his recliner while Carol and Lil still sat at the kitchen table talking quietly about the copied pages.

"There's a fresh pot of coffee," Carol said.

"Just what I need—more caffeine," Max muttered.

Carol got out a yellow legal pad and some highlighters. "Let's get a few notes on what we found, and then I need to go to bed."

Bob stirred and came back in the kitchen but looked like he could barely keep his eyes open. "How did the reverse thievery go?"

Tess told them about the sounds they heard.

"Was it that squirrel?" Lil asked.

Tess shook her head. "Not unless he was wearing large-sized shoes. We definitely heard footsteps."

Carol scratched her head. "How odd. Would they know who you were?"

Tess shrugged. "We didn't talk much and then only whispered. It was spooky."

"I *hope* they can't identify you" Carol answered

Max took a stack of papers and a highlighter. "Whoever it was obviously shouldn't have been there either, so even if they recognized either of us, they couldn't say anything without exposing their own guilt. Let's get this done. First, did anyone find any references to our family?"

"Not me," Carol said.

Lil shook her head, and so did Tess. Max looked at Bob.

"Uh, no. So that should clear all of us, once the sheriff has a look at the manuscript. Unless you found something?"

"I didn't. But that doesn't clear us. If any of us *thought* there was something in there, that's enough for motive."

"Sure. But that's true of anyone. The suspects certainly aren't limited to the people mentioned in the memoir."

"So, what are we looking for then?" Tess asked.

"Anybody else that's mentioned, especially in a negative way."

Lil held up a page. "He talks about that new editor here—Gomar? Dutch says he was reluctant to sell to him at first because he didn't have any references."

Carol said,"I thought he worked for a big paper in Chicago?"

"He apparently did—they confirmed that much but wouldn't give him a reference."

"Odd," Max said. "Sounds like there's something behind that. What else?" She wrote Charlie Gomar's name down on a blank sheet of a legal pad and printed "Suspects" at the top, underlined three times.

"How about Cecil Ridley? Anyone find his name?" Bob said.

They all shook their heads. Max tapped the pad with her pen. "I wouldn't expect to, though. If Dutch was going to expose the deal Dad made, Cecil would *want* that to happen. The only motive he could have would be to throw the blame on us. Nothing that would be in Dutch's book."

Lil said, "What about Donnie's buddies? It seems like they must have had something to do with placing Donnie 'at the scene,' as they say. Any of them have a motive? I don't remember anything that would tie J.P. in."

"Didn't Pete Murphy's dad work for your dad?" Tess asked.

Carol rubbed her forehead. "Bill Murphy was the head of marketing. He and Dad were best friends. They served together in North Africa and Italy during the War. And Bill retired very comfortably a few months before Dad sold the company. Pete would have no reason to hold a grudge."

"We should check out J.P. Prentiss then. And maybe he knows how Donnie ended up in Dutch's car. He had to have some way to get back from the lake."

"Junie Coonley is mentioned on the pages I looked at — not in connection with any affair, but questioning her campaign for mayor," Bob said.

Max nodded and added Junie's name to the list. "Interesting. What other names? Let's just get the list done and then I need to get to bed."

Chapter Nine

Harsh light filtered through the blinds in the pleasant guest room, striking Max's head on the pillows. She groaned and threw her arm up over her eyes. She shifted the arm a bit peeking at the intrusion. It must be late. She was usually up long before the sun. She rolled over to check her watch on the nightstand.

The movement, slow and deliberate as it was, shot a pain up her back. Her first thought was a heart attack or similar dreaded event that lurked in the background of most seventy-something's minds. Then she remembered her escapades of the night before. What was she thinking, crawling in a window? Or more accurately, being stuffed and pushed through a window? An old rotting window with rough edges. Onto a hard counter several feet from the floor. Ugh.

She gingerly sat up and swung her feet over the side of the bed. She leaned forward on her hands, thinking about making the supreme effort to get up, when a black-and-white photo in a gold frame on the nightstand caught her eye. She picked it up and held it to one of the errant sunbeams. Four little girls in identical plaid dresses, wayward curls, and barrettes protectively surrounded a toddler boy in a matching plaid shirt and shorts. Max, the tallest and her brown hair straighter than the others, rested her hand on Donnie's head. Lil, on the other side, had her hand on one shoulder. Sharon and Carol kneeled on either side, each holding on to one of Donnie's hands. Donnie, for his part, looked like he would do anything to escape.

Max smiled sadly and set the picture back on the table. That photo pretty much summed up what was wrong with Donnie. No wonder he had always been so rebellious. She thought of Donnie now sitting in jail, and stood with effort. Some light stretches helped. She picked up her linen pants off a chair and examined with regret the three-corner tear in the thigh.

A tap at the door preceded Lil's voice. "Max? We're leaving for church in about 45 minutes. Are you going?"

Max opened the door, pushing her hair back behind one ear with the other hand. "No. Probably not. I don't —" She looked at the disappointment on Lil's face. "Forget it. Sure, I'll go. We need to put up a united front."

Lil brightened. "Carol's got fruit and rolls downstairs." She grinned. "And strong coffee, of course. You look like you need it."

"Thanks. I'll be down in a minute." She closed the door and grabbed her toiletry bag to head to the bathroom. Fifteen minutes later, she had scrubbed her face, brushed her hair and teeth, and donned black cotton slacks with a black-and-white striped top. A quick glance in the hall mirror met her fairly low appearance standards.

So it was doubly gratifying to reach the kitchen and have Bob glance up from the Sunday paper with a low whistle. "Lookin' pretty sharp, there." He grinned and then added, "For an old lady."

She swatted his shoulder as she passed to get her coffee. "I'm only one year older than you. Not even that. Where are the girls?"

"Girls? The other old ladies you're referring to are out on the patio." He then covered his head with the paper and continued chuckling.

"Honestly. Men! No wonder I got divorced." Max took her coffee outside. The sunny patio glimpsed through the side porch windows lost some of its appeal when she opened the door into a steamy, sultry morning.

"Whoa," she said.

"Yeah, not as pleasant as yesterday." Carol pulled another chair up to the umbrella table. "Looks like there might be storms brewing over in the Dakotas."

Lil tore chunks off a large cinnamon roll, licking her fingers after each bite. "You didn't get a roll? These are fantastic! Carol must have gotten all of Mom's baking talent."

Max raised her cup. "I will in a minute. Don't rush me. This is all I need right now." She shifted in her chair and groaned.

Lil couldn't repress a little smile. "Haven't been doing your breaking-and-entering exercises lately?"

"Shut up. The worst part is that I don't know if we learned much from that manuscript. Maybe his murder was about something else."

"Annie called this morning," Carol said. "She stopped to visit Donnie earlier. The lawyer did see him last night and is going to try to raise bail by tomorrow."

"Good. He probably hasn't learned anything but it may be too late for that. I'll stop and see him after church."

Lil grew serious. "We need to talk to Donnie's friends and find out what transpired that night. Especially, how did Donnie get into town?" She stood and picked up her cup and plate. "I need to go finish getting ready."

Max followed her in to get a bowl of fruit and a roll. The humid morning was not the best time to eat a frosted roll outside, but it tasted great and the fruit hit the spot. She was putting her dishes in the dishwasher and washing her hands when Carol came back in the kitchen. Max heard the walker clomping across the floor.

"Bob and I would like to put up Donnie's bail. I don't know what the lawyer has in mind, but you know Mom and Dad would be disappointed in us for letting him sit there."

Max sighed. "If they had been more disappointed in *him* and done something about it, he wouldn't be in this fix. But I understand—it's probably gone on long enough."

Carol put her hand on Max's shoulder. "I know you mean well and he is spoiled rotten, but he *might* have learned something."

Max smiled at her. "Let's hope. So, are we coming back here before the picnic?"

"Sure. We'll have time and we don't have to take anything. The Band Parents are providing all the food for $10 apiece. I want to change clothes and we should throw in the lawn chairs, I guess."

"Great."

ST. JOHN'S LUTHERAN CHURCH was a plain brick building with white trim and a slim steeple. A decade or so earlier, it had replaced the old gray green board-and-batten structure that Max and her siblings had attended as children. Max and Bob got on either side of Carol to help her up the wide steps.

"I miss the old place," Max said. "It was so … quaint."

"This is air-conditioned," Bob said.

"And there're no mice," Carol added.

"I suppose."

As they entered, Lil pointed out the soft-toned stained glass windows to Max. "Those are the windows Dad paid for. Remember, you were doing that exchange thing in England when they had the dedication."

"Wow," Max said. "They're beautiful. The photos didn't do them justice. But they're not really religious, are they?"

"Depends on your definition," Carol said. "God's creation." The windows depicted Minnesota birds, trees, and flowers. In one, a loon, the state bird, floated among cattails. In another, a cardinal rested on a pine bough, and in a third a chickadee nestled in colorful winterberry branches.

"They're really breathtaking," Max said.

Carol pointed out Annie and the rest of the family in pews toward the front on the left side. They joined the group, just as the organist began playing.

Max no longer attended church regularly but she found comfort in the old bits of ritual that persisted through time. She wondered what her parents would be saying about Donnie if they were still around. She wondered if Donnie ever would grow up. And she wondered who killed Dutch Schneider. However, by the time the service ended, she had regained a little balance and inner peace.

As they filed out, people stopped her and the others or touched her arm to greet them or reintroduce themselves. A few gave sideways or scornful looks but most were warm and welcoming.

Max fished in her bag for her keys. "I'm going to stop to see Donnie. I'll tell him about Bob and Carol's offer," she said to Lil.

"Do you want me to go with you?"

"Not necessary. I won't be long because I want to change clothes and the picnic starts at noon, doesn't it?"

"Yeah, Carol's got our tickets so I'll just wait for you at the house?"

"Great." Max got in her sporty little car and laid just enough tire to impress a couple of teenaged boys standing by the curb.

Lil shook her head and shrugged at Carol. "She'll never change either."

THE LAST TWENTY-FOUR HOURS had transformed Donnie. For one thing, he was now sober, and Max wasn't sure when she had last seen him that way. Oddly, he looked more crestfallen and yet spoke with more confidence.

"Thanks for coming, Max. I wouldn't blame you for just—you know—throwing up your hands."

"Did the lawyer come last night?"

He nodded. "About suppertime."

"Had he been able to find out anything about what evidence they have?"

"Mainly that I was passed out in Dutch's car. He was stabbed with part of an old antenna but that could belong to anybody."

"What about your friends? J.P or Pete? Have they been in to see you?"

Donnie shook his head and his shoulders drooped. "Some friends, huh?"

"Have the cops interviewed them?"

"I dunno."

Max stood up. "Well, I'm going to track them down. *Someone* must have brought you back into town. Bob and Carol are going to post your bail. You should be out sometime this afternoon or tomorrow morning latest."

Relief flooded his face. "Thank you." And he hung his head.

Chapter Ten

Century Park was at the north end of the main highway through Castleroll. It included the city pool, a couple of baseball diamonds, and a fairly new skate park in one corner. But towering maples and ash trees and ancient spreading oaks dominated the bulk of it. Two timber and stone shelters stood near the road, with more picnic tables scattered through the trees. A May pole in one clearing fluttered with ribbons.

"I wonder if they still have the Solstice Sweethearts dance around the pole."

Max felt sure that Lil was trying to remind her that she was the only Jacobsen daughter that hadn't been a Solstice Sweetheart. "Yeah, yeah. Who cares?"

"I'm sorry. I didn't mean—" Lil looked so sorry that Max relented.

"I know you didn't. Just testy today I guess."

Lil didn't respond to that but peered out the window at glimpses of the sky between the trees. "They might be lucky to pull this picnic off before it rains."

Max nodded. "Feels like serious stuff—the air's so heavy."

Parking lots overflowed, but Max found a spot along side one of the park roads and slipped the Studebaker in. Access to the Midsummer Picnic area was controlled by a system of wooden sawhorses and snow fence with one opening, where three people took tickets at a long table.

Everyone headed to a huge green-and-white striped tent in a clearing where a line of people snaked out into the grounds. Lil's daughter Georgiann was already in line and waved at them.

"Aunt Sharon has a couple of tables staked out for us on the other side of the tent."

"Great," Lil said. "We'll get in line. As I recall, 'budging' was never tolerated at this picnic. I don't imagine that has changed."

Georgiann laughed. "Probably not."

THE TENT HELD LONG TABLES laden with farm and garden bounty. Three serving tables each held roasters of barbecued beef and chicken, huge vats of potato salad and coleslaw, fancy-cut watermelon halves filled with fruit, and relish trays.

Volunteers, including Bonnie Johnson Webb, stood behind the tables, serving people and urging them to take more. Bonnie gave Max a brilliant smile and told her how glad she was to see her again.

Some people are just too nice for their own good.

On another table, a feast for the sweet-toothed waited with servings of pie and cake arranged on pastel paper plates. The line moved quickly through the main dishes but bottlenecked at the dessert table as people agonized between cherry and Dutch apple pie or 'icebox dessert' and 'I'm sure those are Ardis Munson's lemon bars.'

Lil mumbled about her diet while they balanced plates, flatware, and drinks and wove their way through the boisterous crowd. Max told her to get over it; she'd been on the same diet for forty years and it hadn't mattered.

Georgiann stood at their table, waving them over. Sharon and Harold slid down to make room for them.

Carol leaned across the table to yell over the din. "Did you see Donnie?"

Max nodded. "He looked and acted a lot better than yesterday. I told him about your generous offer. I could tell he really appreciates it."

"There's J.P. Prentiss," Bob said, with a full mouth and pointing with his fork. He swallowed and wiped his mouth. "Should I go ask him if he knows anything about how Donnie got back to town Friday night?"

"Yes!" Carol said. "He might be more likely to answer you than one of us." She indicated her sisters.

He grinned and got up. "You ladies *are* pretty scary."

They all watched as Bob waylaid a middle-aged man with a blond buzz cut and a small paunch under his Twins tee shirt. The men shook hands and exchanged a few comments. J.P. shook his head in answer to all of Bob's questions. After a few more words, Bob slapped J.P. on the shoulder and let him continue to a table with his plate.

"Didn't look like that gained much," Carol said, as he climbed back over the picnic table bench.

Bob returned to his chicken. "He says when he left the lake Friday night, Donnie was still there. J.P. thought he was just going to crash on the couch in Pete's trailer."

Max grabbed at her plate as a gust of wind tried to scoop it up. A faint rumble of thunder accompanied the wind. They looked up at the sky.

"After we eat, I'm going to take a run out by the lake and see if I can find Pete Murphy. You haven't seen him here today, have you?" Max asked Bob.

"No, but you might get caught in a deluge. Your little toy car would just float away."

"You're jealous and you know it. Do you know where his trailer is?"

"In the old campground at the west end of the lake. It's all permanent sites now. The county supervisors have tried to get rid of it without much luck. Pete's trailer is painted bright pink."

"Pink?"

"He had an argument with his neighbors about a political sign he had in his yard a couple of years back, so in retaliation he painted the trailer pink."

Lil put down the chicken leg she had been delicately picking at. "Is that a symbol of something?"

Bob shook his head. "He said it was the gaudiest color the feed store had that would stick to his trailer. He has an old yellow VW parked next to it."

"Wow," Max said. "Shouldn't be hard to spot."

Annie got up from the table, collected the plastic silverware that Paige and Garth were using for a sword fight and stacked their plates. "I'm going to take the kids over to the bouncy house before it storms. You be careful, Aunt Max!"

Lil leaned over to whisper, "Good thing she doesn't know what you were up to last night."

Max glared at her. "Hush."

"What were you up to last night?" Sharon asked.

Max pretended she didn't hear the question and concentrated on her lemon chiffon pie, raving about its qualities. She was just finishing the pie, keeping an eye on the sky, and an ear to the distant rumbles, when Tess walked by.

"I think there's a city ordinance against this many Jacobsens in one place."

"No doubt. Did you get fed yet?"

Tess rubbed her stomach. "I shouldn't have to eat for a week."

"I'm just about to take a ride out to the lake to try to talk to Pete Murphy. Want to come?"

She gave a sly smile. "Why not? I'll just go tell Roger."

"Who's Roger?"

"My husband. I guess we didn't talk much about that last night." She winked. "Be right back."

Max finished her pie and glanced at Lil. Her sister's expression said she was hurt at being left behind again. Oh, hell.

"Do you want to come?"

Lil brightened. "If you don't care."

"Well, no breaking and entering this time." She glanced around quickly to see if anyone was listening. It didn't seem so. She got Carol's attention and told her their plans.

"We're going to go see about getting Donnie out," Carol said. "If we do, we'll bring him back to the house. He can sleep on the couch. No going back to the motel."

"Good plan. We'll see you later."

Tess came back and they headed for Max's car. Thunder still rumbled in the distance, and the clouds hung heavy above them.

Max wiped her forehead with a tissue. "I would welcome a storm if it would break this heat." When they reached the car, she cranked up the air conditioning full blast.

"Did this car come with AC?" Tess asked.

"I had it installed. Lil and I use it a lot in the summer for trips and Lil doesn't want her 'do' to droop."

"That's not fair," Lil said. "You don't like the heat either."

"Whatever."

They headed out of town on the blacktop leading to the lake. Cattail Lake was one of the ten thousand lakes that Minnesota license plates bragged about. It was small and popular with the local fishermen for fishing and teenagers for beer parties. The old campground—now trailer park—adjoined a small picnic area. About half way there, giant raindrops splattered the car with such force and suddenness that Max jumped. The thunder that had been threatening now crashed around them.

"Holy Moly!" Max leaned forward to peer between the wiper slashes. "I can barely see the road. I'm going to pull over until this lets up."

She spotted a field turnout just ahead on the right and pulled the car over. They sat listening to the thunder and watching the wipers fruitlessly trying to keep up with the deluge. Lightning cracked often enough that they quit jumping at the sound.

Max said, "Tess, Bob talked to J. P. Prentiss today at the picnic. He claims that Donnie was still at Pete's trailer when he went home Friday night. That he thought he was going to stay over night."

"I doubt if any of them were in any shape to give any reliable information," Tess said.

"Probably not."

The rain let up as quickly as it had started and Max pulled back out onto the road. Another crack of lightning came as she got up to speed, followed in a split second by a ping at the front driver's side of the car.

"What was that?" Lil asked. "Is it hailing?"

Max peered out. "No. Something hit the bumper or the fender." Another ping made her jump as the lightning had failed to do.

Tess grabbed for the dashboard. "What the—?"

"I think we're being shot at," Max said, between clenched teeth. One more ping seemed to come from the back end. Max sped up. Tess and Lil gripped their door handles and searched the passing area frantically.

"Why would anyone shoot at us?" Lil gasped.

"Why is *any* of this happening?" Max hunched over the steering wheel while the other two slid down in their seats. The rain continued, not as hard, and the rumbles of thunder came from the east as the storm moved on. The silence in the car increased the tension as they strained to here any more pings on the car.

The twists and dips in the road, shrouded by overhanging trees, required more vigilance. Bob was right. This was a dumb idea. Another one.

They finally reached the lake, and Max drove slowly around the campground/trailer park. Even though the rain had lessened, it still dripped enough to discourage anyone from being outside.

Lil pointed toward the lakeside. "I see it. Only pink trailer out here."

As Bob mentioned, a yellow VW bug sat outside the door.

When Max had parked, she got out and walked around the front of her car. Tess and Lil followed, sneaking looks at their surroundings for anyone who might be a threat.

"Look. Here's a new dent on the bumper and a bigger one on the fender."

"Maybe some kids were throwing rocks?" Lil said hopefully.

"I don't know, but I'll have the sheriff check it out."

Tess asked, "Do you want to go in by yourself, or should we come too?'

"I'll be fine—," Max started and then changed her mind. "You know what? Let's all go. If he does tell me anything important, I want witnesses. Besides, I think we should stick together."

Max grabbed her water bottle from the makeshift holder. Interrogation could be thirsty work. They trooped up to the stoop, and Max rapped on the door. They were about to give up when she heard shuffling inside and the door opened a crack.

A man peered out. His dark hair was wet and disheveled, his eyes baggy and his skin pockmarked. He wore loose green shorts and a disreputable gray tee shirt with some saying about hogs.

"Pete Murphy?" Max asked.

He nodded.

"You may not remember me. I'm Donnie Jacobsen's sister Maxine, and this is my sister Lil and our friend Tess Robinson."

Pete said, "I know Tess. Haven't seen you two in ages, though."

"Can we come in? We wanted to ask what you know about Donnie's whereabouts Friday night."

"Um, sure." He looked around behind him as if he didn't know what was there. "It's kind of a mess. I just got up." But he opened the door wider and they entered.

Pete grabbed some clothes off the couch and a stack of books from a wooden chair. The trailer living space didn't seem dirty, but it was messy. "Have a seat."

Max took the chair while Lil and Tess sat on the couch. Pete remained standing.

Max took a deep breath and began. "I'm sure you are aware of Donnie's predicament?" She waited until he nodded and then continued. "Our problem is that he doesn't remember much of anything that happened Friday night after he left our sister Carol's house. He thinks he was out here with J.P. and you."

"Yeah, he was. J.P. brought him out."

"But J.P. says he didn't take Donnie back to town."

Pete shrugged and ran his hand through his tangled hair, giving him a startled appearance. "Donnie said he was going to sleep on my couch, but he passed out in the yard, and we just left him there. The next morning when I got up and Donnie wasn't in here, I just assumed he was still outside. I didn't know until about ten that he was gone."

"What did he talk about?" Lil asked. "Was he upset?"

Pete shoved his hands in his pockets and glanced out the window. He shuffled his feet and looked back at her.

"Yee-aah, he was." He fidgeted and looked at his feet. "He went on and on about Dutch and how much damage Dutch's book could do to your family's reputation."

Max said. "It couldn't be damaged much more than it already is. And Donnie doesn't even live here any more."

"That's what we tried to tell him." He gave the women a pleading look. "But—I had to tell Sheriff Burns when he asked what Donnie talked about. If I didn't, and J.P. did, I could be in a world of trouble."

"I understand," Max said, although she didn't think it would be all that serious if he had kept his mouth shut. "So you don't have any idea how he got back to town?"

Pete shrugged. "He could've walked, I guess. It's about two-and-a half or three miles."

Lil cocked her head. "Was he in any shape to walk that far?"

"I didn't think so. Maybe someone picked him up?"

Max got up. "Well, thanks for your time. I'm kind of surprised to find you still around. Didn't you go out east to college?"

"Yeah, Dartmouth, but just two years. Then Dad lost everything with a bad investment. I dropped out and got a job." He held the door open for them.

Max took a swig from her water bottle and snapped the cap back on. "I'm sorry to hear that. Was that after your dad retired?"

"Yeah, and by then the Jacobsen plant was sold. Otherwise, he probably would have gone back to work."

Max grabbed the railing to help herself down the rickety steps, hoping her knees didn't give out. "Thanks again. We're hoping Donnie gets out on bail sometime today."

"Um, good. Glad to hear that."

Max swung the bottle by its strap as they walked toward the Studebaker. "He wasn't much help." The bottle slipped out of her hand and rolled under the yellow Volkswagon.

"Crap!" She crouched down to avoid getting the knees of her pants muddy. The bottle had rolled into a large puddle under the car, but she managed to reach it by stretching to her limit. She pulled her arm back and noticed a streak of mud or grease across her sleeve. At this rate she was going to have to go shopping—not her favorite pastime.

"Help me up." She held her hand up. Tess gripped it and pulled her to her feet. She straightened her clothes and looked around. The lot exhibited the same messiness as the inside of the trailer. A busted bike, a couple of oil cans and an overflowing garbage can did nothing for curb appeal. But, in spite of the low hanging clouds, the lake still provided a lovely view.

"Bill Murphy would be very disappointed in his son. Of course, Dad would feel the same about Donnie." They reached her car and she looked again at the dents in it.. This trip was one disaster after another.

Chapter Eleven

THEY RETURNED TO TOWN and Max dropped Tess off at her home. Then she drove to the sheriff's office.

Sheriff Burns was just straightening his desk preparing to leave. He looked up as Max and Lil walked in.

"Your sister already picked'im up," he said, with a slight smile.

"Thank you, but that's not why we're here. We took a drive out to the lake after the picnic, and I think someone shot at us." Max waved her hand at the open door. "They hit my car. Would you take a look?"

Burns gawked at them. "*Shot* at you? How do you know?"

"We heard something hit the car. I thought maybe you could tell. I'll need to file a police report for my insurance."

"If someone was shooting at you, there's more serious issues than your insurance. Show me."

He followed them out to the car. Sheriff Burns' eyes widened.

"Wow! An old Studebaker? What year is this?"

"'50," Max said, caressing the front fender.

"Beautiful." He admired the sleek design with the wrap around rear window. "Where do you think you got hit?"

Max showed him.

"You sure it wasn't rocks being thrown up from the road?" the sheriff asked.

"I'm not sure of anything. It only happened in one place. If it was loose gravel, it would have been more than that."

"Maybe—maybe not. Normally, I would be inclined to write it off as gravel, but you've had kind of a rough weekend. Somebody's not happy you're here, so we'll check it out." He bent over the dent again. "Could have been done by a 45. Since it didn't leave a hole, it was probably something that shoots a large diameter relatively slow-moving bullet like 45 caliber model 1911. They've been made by pretty much every manufacturer that has been making guns since they were introduced back in 1911."

"I don't know anything about guns," Max said.

"Been a standard sidearm for officers in the military—lot of 'em around. Like I said, I'll do some checking. You didn't hear any shots?"

"No, but it was during the storm, and there was a lot of thunder and lightning."

He narrowed his eyes. "Why were you headed to the lake during a storm like that?"

Whoops. Max knew that would raise questions and let it slip anyway. "Well, we went out to talk to Pete Murphy. He and Donnie were friends and—"

"I know who he is and I had already interrogated him."

"He told us that."

He shook his head. "Let's get a report filed on the damage for your insurance." He turned and headed back into the office but asked over his shoulder, "Did you learn anything?"

"Not really," Lil said.

"I didn't think so. They either were all really out of it and don't remember anything or they're all in cahoots to protect Donnie."

Max wisely held her tongue.

It was late afternoon when Max pulled into Carol and Bob's driveway and parked her car to the side of Carol's. The sun had finally emerged from the clouds, but had disappeared behind the house, leaving the east-facing patio in shade. Most of the family had gathered there. Some had already left; Gary and Sheri's motorhome was gone from its spot beside the barn.

Sharon and Bob were bringing out trays of drinks and snacks. The children and Rosie were chasing each other around the yard. Rosie broke away from the games when she heard Max's car and raced up to greet her.

Carol, Harold, Ernie, and Kim were all on the patio surrounding Donnie. He turned as they approached and walked to them, giving both of his sisters a hug. Rosie stood by, expectantly awaiting attention

As Max stepped back from her brother, she looked down and noticed an ankle bracelet. She pointed down and raised her eyebrows in question.

"They're not saying I'm no longer a suspect yet. I'm definitely at the top of the list."

Carol handed Max a glass of wine. "Sit. What did you find out? Anything?"

"Not much. Seems like they all claim amnesia. We did have a weird incident on our way out there, though." She told them about the possible shooting as she scratched Rosie's back. That got the attention of even Sharon's granddaughter Chelsea, who had been ensconced in a papasan chair in the corner, madly texting vital messages to her friends.

Chelsea flipped her curtain of brown hair back. "What? Someone took *shots* at you?"

"We aren't sure. The sheriff thought it was a possibility. None of us should head anywhere alone."

Carol said, "Everyone except you and Lil is leaving tomorrow morning."

"And me," Donnie said glumly.

"Have you called Janet yet?" Max asked him, her tone sharper than she intended.

He shook his head. "My phone was dead when the sheriff returned it. It's on the charger."

"You can use mine." Max held it out to him. "As you know, Janet has tended to rub a lot of us the wrong way, but you've given her good reason to be that way. Call her and apologize."

Donnie took the phone and looked ready to protest but caught Max's glare. "Okay," he said and went around the corner of the house.

Sharon looked at Max in shock. "Wow. Not even an argument. Maybe he's growing up."

"Don't get your hopes up."

Carol took a seat beside Max. "Pete Murphy couldn't tell you anything?"

"Not really. Couldn't or wouldn't--not sure which. Either all three were wasted or they agreed not to talk." Max took a sip of her wine. "It's a little hard to swallow, though, that none of them have any idea what happened. There's something a little off about Pete, too. What happened to Bill Murphy, anyway? Is he still around?"

Sharon said, "He committed suicide shortly before Dad died."

"Really? I never heard that. Did he suffer from depression or something?"

"Not that I'd ever heard. I'd lost touch after he retired, and of course I wasn't around here either."

"I'm sure he got a good retirement package," Lil said. "I remember Dad talking about that."

Max held up a finger as she remembered something. "Pete did say that his dad lost everything on a bad investment. He had to drop out of college because of it."

"I'm sure it was either that or get a job to pay his own way. He doesn't have much ambition," Sharon said.

"But he *did* go to work then. At least that's what he said. What does he do now?" Max asked.

Bob said, "He works over in Prairie City but I don't know what he does."

Donnie returned and handed Max her phone. "That wasn't pleasant. She's coming over tomorrow since I can't leave here."

The sisters exchanged chagrinned looks, but Max accepted that it was her own fault for insisting he call his wife. He sat down in the chair he had vacated and took a drink from the glass on the table. It appeared to be iced tea—not his usual beer or whiskey. And it explained why he was being reasonable and more mature than usual.

"Donnie, have you thought any more about how you got back to town Friday night? You surely didn't walk, did you?"

"I don't think I could have."

"We talked to Pete Murphy this afternoon and he claims not to know. Said you were asleep outside when he went to bed. The next morning you were gone. Bob talked to J.P. at the picnic and he says you were both asleep when he left." Max waited for Donnie to fill in some blanks.

"You sound like you don't believe Pete," Donnie said.

"I don't know. What do you think?"

Donnie shrugged. "I haven't seen him much in years. He always seems a little mad at me." He gave a feeble grin. "But then so do you girls."

"With good reason," Lil said. But she smiled as she said it.

Annie's daughter Paige ran up and patted Carol on the shoulder. "Grandma! Can we each have an ice cream bar?"

Carol looked at her watch. "Omigosh! You need to have some supper first and then you can have ice cream bars." She got up. "I'll get some leftovers out. Ernie and Kim picked up some broasted chicken when they came out, and we've got plenty of other stuff. We can talk more about this after we eat."

Max got up too. "There's something really crazy going on here. We need to see if we can figure out these attacks on our family, for one thing. And if there's any connection to Dutch's murder. But food, first."

They all trooped inside to help, even Donnie.

The next hour was happy bedlam. They put their worries aside and jostled one another to get the kids fed or the last corn muffin or a second scoop of potato salad. Insults and jokes flew, wet rags mopped up spills, and dishes clattered. Afterwards, cleanup took another half hour while the younger generation packed up their kids and headed to their night's quarters. Goodbyes and hugs were shared with those who were leaving the next morning, along with instructions to forward any new developments and, above all, to stay safe.

Finally, the four sisters, Bob, Harold, and Donnie gathered back on the patio. Rosie moved from one to another, accepted affection until the giver tired of it and then moved on to the next sucker.

Harold spoke first. "Max is right in what she said earlier. We need to talk about the threats to the family and insist on knowing what the sheriff has found out. He should know by now who came up with that float in the parade. Then there was the incident at the plant, and the shots fired at Max and Lil."

"We don't know for sure that it was shots," Lil said.

"It probably was," said Max.

"What did the sheriff say?"

"That he was more inclined to consider shots because of the other things that had happened," Max said.

It was quiet for a few moments. A full moon rose and only a few clouds remained. Lil pointed out the lightning bugs rising from the nearby bean field like a movie special effect. It was hard to grasp any kind of threat in such a bucolic setting. That is, until Max cursed and slapped a mosquito feasting on her arm. Her bracelets jangled and Rosie, who had collapsed at her feet, jumped up to protect her. Carol passed Max a box of wipes that promised to be more effective.

Max used a wipe to smear her arms and ankles. "You're right, Harold. The float would seem to be the place to start. The people had masks on, but surely that deputy got the license number off the truck."

Carol shook her head. "He was pretty preoccupied with getting the whole thing out of the parade. He might not have had time."

"Well, we need to check. I'll talk to the sheriff first thing tomorrow and also see if he knows any more about who might have locked us in the plant," Max said.

"Remember that the murder and the attacks on us may not be connected," Bob pointed out.

More quiet and firefly watching. Max snapped her fingers. "I just thought of something that bothered me about Pete Murphy. He told us he had just gotten up when we arrived—"

"In the middle of the afternoon?" Sharon interrupted.

"Right. But when we left and I dropped my water bottle—it rolled under his car—there were puddles under there. The ground was soaked and muddy—he must have parked the car there after the rainstorm. His hair was wet, too."

"Are you saying that he was the one who shot at us?" Lil asked.

"Not necessarily. I don't think he could have gotten back there that fast. The point is, he was lying when he said he had just gotten up. Why, I don't know. So maybe he was lying about Friday night as well."

Bob leaned forward and clasped his hands. "But we had already eliminated him as a suspect, because we didn't know of a motive. Did anyone see his or Bill Murphy's name in the manuscript?"

Sharon sat up. "What manuscript?"

"Oops," Bob said. He turned to Sharon, Harold, and Donnie. "Let's just say that we were able to get a look at

Dutch's manuscript and search for any names who might be threatened by Dutch publishing that book."

"How—?" Harold began, but Bob held up his hand. "I'm not at liberty to go into detail."

Right, Max thought, because then he would be the next murder victim.

Donnie had sat quietly through this discussion. Now he looked at Max, Lil, and Carol. "What did you do?" His voice carried a touch of admiration along with accusation.

Max waved a hand. "Don't worry about it. It sounded like that manuscript might very well be behind his murder. Necessity is the mother of invention, or whatever."

"But, how—?"

Lil put her hand up. "Don't ask. Seriously, it's better that you don't know."

Donnie sat back and took a long drink of his iced tea, but continued to look at his sisters with something akin to disapproval. Ironic, Max thought, how quickly roles can be reversed. For once Donnie was not the one with questionable actions as far as the theft of the manuscript was concerned, but only because he had been sitting in jail at the time.

Lil said, "To get back to your question, Bob, I didn't see anything about the Murphys in the pages that I looked at."

"Me either," Carol said.

Max shook her head. "Nor did I, but maybe Tess did."

"What does Tess have to do with this?" Sharon asked, frowning.

"She helped." Max didn't elaborate on helped with what. "So Bill Murphy retired with a good settlement before the business was sold. We know that for sure?"

"That's what your dad told me," Bob said.

"According to Pete, he lost everything with a bad investment, and then committed suicide. Does anyone know if that's true?" Max looked around at the group.

"He did commit suicide," Sharon said. "I remember hearing about that. But I never heard anything about why."

"But there doesn't seem to be any reason why Pete would hold a grudge against us or Dutch," Lil said.

Harold agreed. "No, there doesn't. So why don't you fill us in on who the other suspects are that you 'happened' upon?"

Max got up. "I made a list. I'll get it."

When she returned, she could tell that Sharon had been pumping Lil and Carol about the manuscript. Sharon quickly shut her mouth with a guilty look when Max stepped back outside.

Carol said, "Maybe we should talk to Beatrice."

Max sat down with her tablet. "I didn't know she was even still alive."

"Who's Beatrice?" Harold asked.

"She was Dad's secretary/business manager for years. Yes, Max, she's alive. She's in the assisted living wing of the nursing home. I don't know how her memory is."

"Wouldn't hurt to try," Max said. "I'm sure she knew more about the business than all of us put together. So we need a plan for tomorrow. We should divide and conquer. We need to talk to Sheriff Burns and Bea. Also the attorney to see what he knows."

"We need to talk to the mayor about the possibility of turning the plant into some kind of community center — see how the city feels about that and how much help they might be willing to give us," Carol said. "I really want to get something going with that memorial money."

Max waved her hand. "That isn't the urgent issue right now. We — wait a minute. Isn't the mayor that Junie Coonley?"

Carol grinned. "Yes, it is."

"Okay, two birds with one stone. I'll talk to the sheriff and the mayor. You take Bea and Larsen. Lil can go with you."

"Good thing we have you to tell us what to do," Lil said, earning a dirty look from her sister.

With a plan in hand, it was time for bed.

Chapter Twelve

THE NEXT MORNING after breakfast, Max in her car and Lil and Carol in Carol's car, caravanned to town. Bob asked Donnie to help him with field work, and Donnie readily agreed. His wife, Janet, wasn't due to arrive until after lunch.

The women stopped first at Annie's to say goodbye to Sharon, Harold, Kim, Ernie and Chelsea. To their surprise, Chelsea was still in shorts and a sleep tee shirt, her hair a nest of tangles, and she lounged in one of the kitchen chairs.

Annie gave her mother a wry smile. "Chelsea wants to hang around a while. She said she would help out with the kids."

Chelsea looked up and said, "Yeah." But her enthusiasm was somewhat lacking.

Carol raised her eyebrows at Annie, but didn't say anything.

Sharon and Kim both looked apologetic. "So where are you off to today?" Sharon asked.

Max explained about their planned visits to the sheriff, the mayor, the nursing home, and the lawyer. Chelsea perked up. "Can I go?"

Max found Chelsea an unpleasant child to be around and was not happy about the idea, but Carol said, "Sure, but you have to get dressed."

Annie led Chelsea upstairs to arrange a room for her. Sharon said, "Thank you. I hope she isn't a nuisance, but she hardly ever shows interest in anything." She paused and grinned. "Especially riding around with a bunch of old ladies."

"But I have a cool car," Max said. "Of course she wants to go with me." And then wondered what made her say that.

Sharon gave them all hugs. "Thank you again. Call me if there's problems. I don't want Annie to have to deal with any trauma."

"We will. She should be fine. She doesn't know anyone here," Carol said.

Lil added, "New playgrounds, new playmates?"

Sharon nodded. "They do recommend that."

Chelsea joined them a few minutes later, her phone gripped in her hand. Her grandmother said to her, "Now, don't let these ladies lead you astray. They don't have the best reputations."

Chelsea squeezed out an 'Oh, sure' smile. "I'll be careful."

Sharon turned to her sisters. "She thinks I'm kidding."

"I'm insulted." Lil put her hand on her chest. "But I'll get over it. Let's go—we have a busy day ahead."

Lil put Carol's walker back in the trunk of Carol's car. After they left for the nursing home, Chelsea took the passenger seat in the Studebaker and they were off to the sheriff's office. On the way, Chelsea asked, "I don't mean to be nosey, but why do you care about old records?"

"We're trying to find out who killed Dutch Schneider so Uncle Donnie gets off the hook," Max said.

SHERIFF BURNS was giving instructions to one of his deputies and looked up as they entered.

"I hope I'm not in trouble." He grinned. "You ladies look pretty determined."

"We just need to talk a minute," Max said. "Do you have time?"

He looked at his watch. "I have about fifteen minutes. Let's go back to my office."

They followed him down a narrow hall to a medium sized room, sparsely furnished. He directed them to go on in while he grabbed a chair from an adjoining room.

"Have a seat." He sat at his desk, pushed some papers to one side, and clasped his hands in front of him. "What can I do for you? No more incidents, I hope."

"No, but we're wondering if you've found out anything about the others. Do you have an identification of the truck that pulled that float?" Max asked.

He leaned back in his chair. "No, we don't. We did get film from the security camera at the bank drive up across the street, but they had covered the license plate, and none of my deputies recognized it as being local.

We're putting a request for information on the county website, but I don't know how many actually look at that."

Chelsea said, "Maybe you should put it on Facebook."

The sheriff pointed his finger at her. "Good idea." She grinned.

"Don't you think that the attacks will stop now that most of the family has left town?" asked Max.

Sheriff Burns nodded but looked skeptical. "We hope so. We did find some tire tracks at the plant. Are the vehicles that you drove there still around so that we could compare and see if there're any unidentified ones?"

"I drove," Max said, "and Annie brought her van. Who else?" She looked at Chelsea.

Chelsea had been fidgeting in her chair, perhaps nervous because she wasn't used to being in a place like this without being in trouble. At Max's question, she straightened in her chair, obviously pleased to be asked. "Aunt Carol drove, and the guy who takes care of the place." She blushed a little.

Max smiled. "Trevor Jasper. So they should all be available to check against."

"Good," Burns said. "Do you have your car out here now?"

"Yes," Max said.

"If you'll give me your keys, I'll have Bergman get a reference print." Seeing the look on Max's face, he added, "I will threaten him within an inch of his life if he harms the car. And if you would leave the names of the owners and locations of the other vehicles with Cathy at the desk, I would appreciate it."

Max handed over her keys. "Tell him not to change the seat adjustment or the radio station."

"Will do."

Chelsea giggled. Max gave her a stern look and stood up. "Thank you. We won't take any more of your time." They stopped at the reception desk to leave the requested information and by the time they finished—Cathy was interrupted several times by phone calls—the deputy, Bergman, had just finished driving the little Studebaker along a strip of brown paper leaving a clear pattern of the tire.

"How did you do that?" Max asked the deputy.

"Inked the tire."

"*Ink?*"

He held up his hands. "It should be gone by the end of the day. Won't hurt anything."

"Better not."

"Nice car, though." He grinned.

"Thanks."

THE NURSING HOME was a small, one-story brick building, but with neat landscaping and a warm, welcoming entrance. Carol asked the young woman at the reception desk for Beatrice Borgstad's room number. She gave it to them but informed them that Beatrice had physical therapy appointment scheduled in half an hour. She directed them down the hall to the right.

Most of the doors were closed and hung with artificial wreaths or pages from coloring books taped above the room numbers. Solid wood railings along the walls separated the red and pink flowered wallpaper on the bottom from the pale green paint on the top. The decor hadn't been updated in some time, but it was cozy and no doubt reflected the tastes of many of the residents.

Lil reached room 11 first and found the door standing open. Loud voices projected from the room. Since Carol had seen Beatrice most recently, Lil stepped aside to let her enter first.

"Bea? It's Carol Jacobsen Harstad. Remember me?"

Beatrice sat in a lounge chair by the window, studiously watching a TV mounted on the wall above a chest of drawers. A talk show in progress blared with laughter, cheers, and screams. Beatrice was small and stooped with wispy grey hair framing her face. She looked around as if she wasn't sure if Carol's voice came from the TV show or somewhere else in the room. Finally her eyes came to rest and focus on the two women in the doorway.

"Oh! Carol? Jacobsen, you say?"

Carol walked forward and bent over Beatrice, taking her hand. "Yes. How are you? Do you remember my sister Lillian?"

Beatrice sat up straighter. "Of course! How are you girls?"

Lil laughed and took Bea's other hand. "We're fine, but no one has called us girls for a long time."

Bea beamed. "How wonderful to see you. Can you stay a bit? Have a seat?" She picked up a remote, turned off the TV, and indicated a beige love seat next to a small table with two chairs. A single bed and a kitchenette with an apartment sized refrigerator took up the rest of the room.

"We can, just for a bit." Carol pulled one of the chairs out to face her and Lil perched on the love seat. "We were told you have physical therapy scheduled soon."

Bea peered at a large clock on the wall. "Yes, I suppose I do. But we can visit a bit. Tell me where you all live now and what you are doing."

Lil did, keeping an eye on the clock. Then Carol said, "Bea, we have a few questions about the last years of our father's company."

"Yes?" She looked a little confused. "That was a long time ago."

"I know it was," Carol said, "but I don't know if you heard about Dutch Schneider's death?"

"Oh, awful, awful. They said he was murdered?" Bea clenched her hands and shook her head. "A murder here in Castleroll. Awful."

"Yes, it is," Lil said, "and our brother Donnie is being charged for it. We know he isn't guilty so we're trying to help him."

Bea put her hand on her sunken chest. "Little Donnie? Oh, no. That isn't right."

Lil was not surprised at Bea's reaction. She had always kept special treats in her desk drawer for Donnie whenever he showed up at the plant as a child. It had always been clear that he was the woman's favorite.

Carol tried to keep the focus. "Do you remember when Dad sold the company if there was more than one offer?"

Bea turned and glanced out the window. "Let me see." She looked back at them. "Yes, I think there was."

Lil said, "We have been told that there was another offer—a lower one—from someone who promised they would keep the plant open. Do you remember anything about that?"

"I believe that's right. Why?" Bea's voice was soft and nonjudgmental. She might have been discussing the menu for lunch.

"We've been wondering why Dad didn't take that offer. We know he didn't want to close the plant. There are a lot of people in town who are still angry about it. Do you know why he went with the other offer?"

"He needed the money," Bea said immediately, and with conviction.

Carol looked Lil, and Lil blurted "But he wasn't broke or anything. Not even close."

"He lost a great deal of money with a bad investment. He had lots of long meetings with his lawyer and Bill Murphy."

"Bill Murphy?" Carol asked. "Hadn't he retired by that time?"

"Oh, yes. But he came back for these meetings."

"Did Bill talk Dad into the investment? Pete Murphy told us that *his* dad lost everything with some investment."

"I don't know about that. I wasn't privy to the meetings." She sounded a little put out about that.

A cheery voice called from the doorway. "Excuse me, Bea, but are you ready to go to your therapy?" A young woman with long straight brown hair rolled a wheelchair in. Her name tag read 'Laura.'

Bea sat up straighter and smiled. "Yes, dear. I was just visiting with the daughters of my old boss." She turned to the sisters. "I'm sorry, but they are strict about schedules here."

"We understand," Carol said and patted her hand. "Thank you for talking to us."

"One other quick question," Lil said as Laura helped Bea into the wheel chair. "Was Hank Larson the attorney Dad was having those long meetings with?"

"Oh yes, of course. Come back and see me again." Bea lifted her hand in a wave as Laura pushed her chair toward the door.

On the way out, Carol took time to visit with others in the common area whom she knew from church or community activities. They didn't discuss Bea's information until they were back in Carol's car.

"What do you think?" Carol said as they pulled out of the parking lot.

"We need to talk to Hank Larsen. I hate to keep asking this about people we used to know but he's still alive, isn't he? You said he retired."

"He is alive but has dementia real bad. He's in a facility in Prairie City. He won't be helping us."

"What about his son?" Lil asked. "Does he still have the company legal records?"

"As far as I know. No one in the family was given any of them."

Chapter Thirteen

Max got the new city hall location from Cathy, who assured her that the mayor would be there in the mornings.

On their way, Chelsea asked Max, "What does the mayor have to do with all this?"

Max thought a moment before she answered. They hadn't included any of the younger generation in their discussions of Donnie's case and the family secrets. Maybe that was partly responsible for the girl's attitude.

"Well, we're going for two reasons. First, the family needs to decide what to do with that old plant and we have some memorial money we could use to help fix it up for a community center—you know, for weddings and other celebrations. But the city would have to take charge of it. I want to see if there's any interest on their part. Second, Junie Coonley is mentioned in the manuscript and may have a grudge against Dutch."

"What's the deal about the manuscript?" Chelsea appeared to be trying to drill into Max's mind.

"We kind of borrowed it for a little bit." Max pulled into the City Hall parking lot. She turned off the key but didn't get out. Instead she turned in her seat to look directly at Chelsea. "You have to promise not to tell a soul."

Chelsea wagged her head, more animated than Max had seen her all weekend.

"Lil and I and a friend broke into the murdered man's apartment Saturday night to get a look at this manuscript Dutch was writing."

Chelsea cocked her head and squinted her eyes. "Whaddya mean, 'broke in'? You broke down a door or something?"

"No, of course we didn't break down the door. We're old ladies, after all. I just crawled in a window and let the others in."

Chelsea's mouth dropped open. "*You* crawled in a window?"

"That's what I said. I'm not *that* old. So there's a connection to Her Honor the Mayor because Dutch mentioned in his book that there might have been some irregularity in her election. Also we heard rumors that she and Dutch were having an affair. Let's go see what we can find out. Remember, mum's the word about the break-in." Max got out of the car.

Chelsea followed her. "*Mum's* the word?"

"That means no spilling the beans. No talking."

"Oh. Okay."

A middle-aged woman held a phone with the mouthpiece covered while she talked animatedly to a young man in a suit. She referred him to a numbered code book in another office and then noticed Max and Chelsea. "Can I help you?"

"We'd like to speak to Mayor Coonley for a few minutes if we could," Max said.

The woman peered at them over her glasses, trying to place them. "May I tell her what this is about?"

"We have a proposal for the old Jacobsen plant."

"What kind of proposal?"

Max gave an exasperated sigh. "I would rather discuss that with her."

The woman shrugged. "I'll see if she's busy." She headed down a long hall.

Chelsea nudged Max and grinned. "Way to go, Aunt Maxine."

"Sometimes you just have to be firm. You'd think this is the city of Chicago the way she acts. I'll bet the mayor hasn't been 'busy' all morning."

The woman soon returned and said grudgingly, "You can go in." She didn't feel it was necessary to lead them, though.

Sure enough, Mayor Coonley had her desk chair swiveled toward the window and watched a young boy chase a small dog on the city hall lawn. Max and Chelsea entered and stood for a moment quietly until Max cleared her throat loudly.

The mayor swiveled back and looked a little annoyed at being interrupted. "What's this about?"

"May we sit?" Max asked.

"Sure." The tone was *If you have to*. They sat.

"I'm Maxine Berra. I was a Jacobsen. This is my great-niece, Chelsea. I'm sure you know the family gathered this weekend for a reunion. One of our purposes was to decide what to do with the old Jacobsen plant. I understand the city has been—concerned, shall we say?—about it sitting there empty"

"I guess."

"We would like to propose donating it as a community center. We have some memorial funds for renovations, but we would turn the ownership over to the city."

Max waited. Junie rotated a pencil between two fingers, tapping the desk. "I'm not sure how the council would feel about that. It would be their decision, of course. There would be liability and upkeep to consider."

"Of course," Max echoed. "What is your sense of how receptive the council might be?"

Junie looked back out the window. "I don't really know."

"Would you give me the contact information for the council members? Maybe we could approach them before we leave town."

"I suppose. You're here for a reunion, you say?"

"It's over. It was this past weekend. I'm sure you heard that there were several threats and actions against the family. We would like to make amends for the bad feelings."

"Threats?" Junie squinted and tried to act surprised, but her manner wasn't convincing.

"Yes, threats. And my brother has been charged—falsely, I might add—with the murder of Dutch Schneider." She watched Junie's face closely. "They seem to think that the family was worried about what might come out in Dutch's memoir, which couldn't be further from the truth."

Junie seemed to blanch so Max went on. "I've seen the manuscript, and there is nothing our family would be concerned about."

Now Junie did turn pale. "How did you see it?"

"Oh, Dutch and I have kept in touch for years. He asked me to read it." Max waved her hand nonchalantly, hoping Chelsea would keep quiet. In for a penny, in for a pound. "I understand you and Dutch were *quite* good friends? I'm sorry for your loss." She thought she heard Chelsea snicker but didn't want to look at the girl.

"Why—more like casual friends, I would say." The mayor paused. "Where is the manuscript?"

"I assume the police have it, which should clear my brother in the next day or so. There were several others more worried than we would be." Max stood up. "We've taken enough of your time. What about the contact information for the council?"

Junie stood also. "Um, Helen, my assistant can give you that. It's also online on the city website."

Max thanked her and ushered Chelsea out the door. Helen readily gave them a list of the council members and their contact information, and turned back to her previous task without a word. Max raised her eyebrows at Chelsea, who giggled, and they headed out the door.

Once outside, Chelsea said, "I don't think you were being quite honest with her. The mayor, I mean."

"No, I wasn't. I was trying to pull a little bluff on her. She's obviously uncomfortable that I have seen that manuscript."

"You didn't mention the election."

"Nope, but I've got her worried."

Chelsea shook her head as they reached the car and grinned. "This is cool."

AFTER THE NURSING HOME, Carol and Lil headed for town and Ted Larsen's law office. Another young receptionist looked at them questioningly as they walked in.

"Can I help you?"

"We just have a quick question for Mr. Larsen. Might he have a few minutes? We're George Jacobsen's daughters."

"Oh! Yes. He's not with anyone right now—let me check." She bounced up and went to a door behind her and tapped. "Mr. Larsen?" She opened the door a crack, nodded, and closed it. "He's on the phone. Do you want to wait?"

"Yes," Lil said. "Maybe you can help us. Do you know if he still has the business files for Jacobsen Antenna?"

The girl looked crestfallen. "I'm sorry. I don't know. My mother is the regular assistant here and is sick today, so I'm just filling in. Like, answering the phone and stuff."

"That's fine. We'll wait and ask him." Carol turned her walker toward one of the client chairs.

"Can I get you some coffee or water or something?" The poor girl was so eager to be useful that Carol said yes, she would take a glass of water. Lil declined and the girl stepped in to a small side room where a counter and sink could be seen.

The women leafed through old magazines for about ten minutes until a middle-aged man in a brown sport coat and Vikings tie stepped out of the inner office. Lil hoped his legal prowess surpassed his sense of style.

"Please come in," he motioned to them.

They introduced themselves. Carol explained their errand.

Ted Larsen took a sip of his coffee and leaned back in his chair. "I'm sure I do still have the records. We haven't done any major purging of files since I took over. What is it you need to know?"

Lil said, "There is anger in town over the sale and closing of the plant, even after all this time. None of us were involved in that process, and we have some questions."

Larsen pulled a notebook and pen over in front of him. "Shoot."

"We have heard that there were two offers—a lower one that guaranteed that the plant would be kept open and a higher one, which Dad accepted. In the normal course of events, there would be nothing surprising about that—it would be considered good business. But Dad felt very strongly about keeping the plant open and its importance to the Castleroll economy. Bea Borgstad, his business manager, told us this morning that he took the higher offer because he desperately needed the money. That doesn't jive with what we know—or thought we knew." She stopped and waited for his reply.

He finished the note he was writing and looked up. "As you probably know, I was not in the practice during those negotiations and my father—well, let's just say his memory is about gone. I don't think he could tell us anything reliable. I haven't ever had cause to look at those records, but I will and see what I can find out.

"Another question has to do with who was involved. Bea told us that Bill Murphy, who had already retired came back for some of the meetings," Lil said.

Larsen jotted on his notebook again. "I'll see if there are records of such meetings. Anything else?"

"I don't think so. Here's a card with my cell number if you find anything out. And thank you for finding a lawyer for our brother." Carol said as she stood.

He stood also and shook their hands. "Glad to be of help."

When they got to the car, Lil pulled out her phone and called Max, who was just leaving City Hall.

"We're done. Do you want to meet for lunch or just go back to the farm?" Lil said.

"Good timing. We just finished too. I'll leave it up to Chelsea." She turned to her great niece. "Lunch out or back to the farm?"

Chelsea was almost giddy. "Lunch out! We need to compare notes."

"Lunch it is," Max said into the phone.

After some discussion, they decided to meet at Nancy's Diner, where they had planned to lunch on Saturday until the events of that morning upset everyone too much.

Chapter Fourteen

On the way to the diner, Max instructed Chelsea to call Annie and update her on their plans. Chelsea reported after she hung up that Annie had just put the baby down for a nap and would not join them at this time.

Carol and Lil had snagged a booth away from most of the lunch crowd. Chelsea and Max slid in and ordered drinks from the waitress, who had appeared immediately at Max's elbow.

Max opened a well-worn menu and said, "Let's order, and then I want to hear first if you found anything out from Bea."

Lil winked at Chelsea and said, "She likes to boss us all around."

"I know," said Chelsea, smiling at Max as she said it.

"Whatever. What's good here, Carol?"

"The BLT panini and the crab cake sandwiches are my favorites."

Max slammed the menu shut. "I like the sound of the crab cakes."

They placed their orders and when the waitress left, Max leaned forward over the table. "Okay. Talk."

"Bea says Dad took the higher offer because he really needed the money," Lil reported.

Max straightened up. "No kidding? That's crazy. I never heard anything like that. Did anyone else?"

Carol and Lil shook their heads. "Furthermore," Carol added, "Bea remembered that Bill Murphy came to the meetings, even though he had retired a couple of years before."

"That is odd."

Chelsea wanted to know who Bill Murphy was and Lil explained.

"Is he related to Pete Murphy?" Chelsea asked.

Max looked surprised. "He was Pete's father. How do you know Pete?"

Chelsea closed her mouth and reverted to her sullen look. She shrugged her shoulders and took a drink of her soda.

Carol fixed a stare on Chelsea. "Chelsea? You haven't been here that often. How do you know Pete?"

"I don't *really* know him. I mean, I've never met him—just heard of him," she finally answered.

"In what context?" Max asked. Chelsea gave her a blank stare. "What did you hear about him?"

"Some kids were talking yesterday at the picnic." She shrugged again and took another drink. "Maybe he deals drugs." Her voice was very soft.

"Chelsea!" Lil said. She put her hand across the table and took Chelsea's. "You didn't buy anything, did you?"

"No, I didn't! Honest! I didn't get a chance. Besides, it's not any worse than breaking in somewhere and stealing stuff." She gave them a defiant little smirk.

"Borrowing," Max said. "And it *is* worse. If we ruin the rest of our lives, that doesn't amount to much. Yours does. If one of us keels over, everyone would be sad for a couple of weeks and then move on. If anything happens to *you*, your parents and many others would never get over it. But thanks for telling us. That might be important."

Lil stared at Max. "*Now* who's been spilling the beans?"

"Yeah, yeah." Max paused while the waitress delivered their sandwiches and then said, 'Did you find out anything at Larsen's office?"

Carol swallowed a bite of her panini and nodded. "They still have the records. Ted is going to see what he can find about the sale and call us. What did you find out?"

Max told them about the lack of identification of the truck from the license plate. "But, they found tire tracks at the plant. They will be getting prints of Annie's van, your car, Carol, and Trevor Jasper's for elimination. Then we had a visit with Her Honor the Mayor."

Chelsea shook off her pout and nodded. "She really acted suspicious."

Carol and Lil smiled at the observation, but Max said, "She's right. Junie *is* worried about that manuscript."

"Aunt Maxine might have fudged a little about what was in it." Chelsea grinned.

"A little," Maxine said. "We got her nervous. Somehow I don't see her doing Dutch in with an antenna though. Seems like with her, the murder would have been more heat of the moment. I can't see her planning ahead to use the antenna."

"Maybe that was a coincidence. It could have just been laying in the alley," Lil suggested.

Max wadded up her napkin and pushed her plate aside. "Maybe. Well anyway, we made some progress. Let's go back to the farm and organize our notes—see what we can come up with."

Carol's phone rang. She looked at the screen. "Bob," she said to the others as she answered. "Hi. We're just about to head out there. What's up?" She listened a few moments, concern growing on her face. "When was this? Okay, we'll be right there." She hung up. "He can't find Donnie. Said he sent him back to the house for some water and he disappeared. He's taken off."

Max stood up and pulled her billfold out of her fanny pack. "That little jerk. When is he ever going to learn?" She laid a couple of bills on the table and picked up her check. "Let's go."

The others followed and they paid for their meals at the cashier's station before hurrying to their cars. To Max's surprise, Chelsea thanked her for the lunch on the way.

As they pulled in the farm yard, Bob was just coming around the corner of the house.

"Did you find him?" Lil called as soon as she got out of the car. Bob shook his head.

They gathered on the patio. "His truck's still here." Carol pointed across the lane. "That's what I can't figure out."

Bob held up a set of keys. "I've kept these. He hasn't even asked about them."

"That ankle monitor won't let him get far. Has the sheriff called?" asked Max.

"No, he hasn't—unless he called the land line. I didn't check the voice mail in there. I'm guessing Donnie's here somewhere trying to get that monitor off," Bob said.

"I doubt if the sheriff would call if Donnie's alarm went off—he'd just head out here," Carol said. "How long has Donnie been gone?"

Bob looked at his watch. "Maybe a half hour or a little more?"

"So if the alarm went off, the sheriff would have been here by now. Donnie *must* still be here somewhere."

"Tell us where you looked and we'll all help," Max said. "If Janet gets here before we find him, it could be worse consequences than from the sheriff."

"Just the house. I thought he might have gone to the basement and fallen on the steps or went upstairs to take a nap. He's nowhere in there."

Max dumped her fanny pack and notebook in one of the patio chairs. "Let's get going. Chelsea, you with me?"

"Sure."

Bob put his hands on his hips. "Okay, why don't you two check the grove and the machine shed? Lil and I'll search the barn and tool shed and Carol, you check the garage."

They spread out to their assigned areas. Max and Chelsea walked toward the grove, a small stand of ash and willow interspersed with wild shrubs. They spread out and walked into the thicket, calling Donnie's name. They could hear the others yelling as well. Mosquitos dive bombed them in the shadows and attacked Max's eyes

"Why would he be hiding?" Chelsea asked, as they met on the other side of the little grove.

"I don't know. He doesn't want to face his wife, maybe, or he thinks he can get the monitor off and escape. I don't know." Max was exasperated by the whole business. Back out in the sunlight, flies took up where the mosquitos had left off.

"Let's go check out the machine shed." Max led the way to the long steel building. A side door stood open and they edged inside, careful not to fall over anything in the dim light. Without windows, only the open door allowed the daylight in. The place smelled of dust and oil. A hulking combine towered over them and other machinery sat in a long row disappearing into the depths of the building.

"Donnie?" Max called. "Are you in here?"

No answer.

"You go around that side and I'll go this way," she said to Chelsea. "Be careful not to trip on anything."

"There's probably a light switch somewhere." Chelsea peered up into the rafters where large fluorescent fixtures could faintly be seen.

"By one of the doors, I suppose, but I don't see one." Max called out again. "Donnie!" She started to move along the wall. Chelsea went the other direction, calling Donnie's name as well.

Max hit her shin on an implement of some sort, and stopped to rub the sore spot. She heard some shuffling from the far end of the building in the opposite direction from Chelsea. She straightened up and listened carefully.

More shuffling, and then a shout. "Max! Get away! Don't come back here!" It was Donnie.

"Donnie? What's the matter? What are you doing?" She ignored his warnings and continued along the wall toward the sound of arguing voices kept low.

To be as quiet as possible, she moved slowly and paused frequently to listen. Suddenly more noise erupted from the back of the building. A young girl's scream—Chelsea! Shouts from Donnie of "No!"

Maxine reached the back and turned the corner. Against the wall, about halfway down the side, Pete Murphy held Donnie around the neck by one arm, the other pointing a gun at Donnie's head. Chelsea stood a few feet on the other side of them, her hands up palms out, in front of her. Pete spotted Max and looked at her in anger. His eyes were wild.

Chapter Fifteen

Max was stunned at first but quickly recovered. "What do you think you're doing, Pete?"

"I want my share. You Jacobsens always run everything. I'm sick of Donnie coming back here and playing Mr. Cool, King of Everything. I want my share!"

The image of Donnie as 'Mr. Cool' almost made Max laugh. Her brother had always been anything but. However, she kept her head.

"What do you mean? Why are you threatening him? Your share of what?"

He threw back his head and laughed. "The money of course. I'm glad you're here. Go tell your sisters that if you want to keep your baby brother alive, I want one hundred thousand dollars in one hour. And that sweet little girl—she stays here too. And no cops."

Max shook her head, trying to play for time, to get her thoughts together. "I don't understand."

"Your family cost me my dad *and* my inheritance."

"That doesn't make sense, Pete. Your dad retired before the company was ever sold. He got a good retirement package."

He started yelling. "No, he didn't. He didn't get anything! I'm not arguing. I told you what I want. Go, before you run out of time!"

Max caught Chelsea's eye. She appeared amazingly calm. "I'll be okay," she said.

"All right. Just stay cool, Pete. I'll see what I can do." Max turned and worked her way back to the door as quickly as she could. Her sore shin made her hobble a little. Outside, the bright sun almost blinded her. She hurried back toward the house where she could see Lil, Carol and another woman on the patio. As she got closer, she recognized Donnie's wife, Janet. As if they needed another complication.

Max waited until she got within speaking distance since she was a little out of breath. "He's in the machine shed," she said. "Pete Murphy's got him." She nodded to Janet.

Janet was a pretty woman, late fifties, with heavy brown hair pulled back in a loose knot and dark-rimmed glasses. However, her looks were marred by the haughty expression she usually wore. She gaped at Max. "What are you talking about?"

"Janet just got here, and we haven't had a chance to tell her what's going on," Carol said. "Janet, Donnie disappeared a little bit ago when Bob sent him in to refill the water jugs. We were afraid he had taken off and were searching for him."

Bob hurried back from the tool shed. "Have you seen Pete Murphy? His car's out behind the machine shed."

"I was just telling them. Pete has Donnie in the shed and he has a gun. He wants money," Max hurried to explain.

Lil looked around. "What about Chelsea?"

"He has her, too." Max's words tumbled over each other. "We split up and she got to them first. It was stupid—I never should have let her out of my sight, but I thought we were only looking for Donnie. I never even considered someone else grabbing him." She was as close to breaking down as her sisters had ever seen her.

Lil put her hand on Max's arm. "We all thought that."

Janet's face softened. "Pete has a gun on Donnie? And Chelsea?" Her eyes filled with tears. Would wonders never cease?

Lil moved to put her arm around Janet. "We'll get him out of there. Bob, are you calling the sheriff?"

Bob who had his phone to his ear, nodded.

Carol started to ask, "What is this about money?" but her phone interrupted her. "Yes, Ted? Thanks for calling, but I'll have to call you back—what?" She covered her other ear and pushed her walker away from the group.

Max told the rest about Pete's demands. "He said an hour." She looked at her watch. "Forty-five minutes now."

"He surely won't harm them when it comes down to it, will he?" Lil said.

Max shrugged. "I wouldn't count on it. He looks crazy. I think he's on something."

"Oh!" Janet choked out a sob and covered her mouth.

Bob had hung up his phone. "The sheriff is on his way. We need to negotiate more time. We can't get that much cash in that time. It'll take longer than that to get to town and back. Will he let me talk to him?"

Max said, "I'd better do it. He would see you as more of a threat than an old lady."

Carol came back to the group. "That was Ted Larsen. He found the records of the meeting about the sale and found out why Bill Murphy was there." She took a deep breath. "I'll make this as short as I can. Bill Murphy had embezzled a lot of money from the company. Dad insisted on his resignation, of course. He didn't get a retirement package but promised he would get another job and pay Dad back if Dad would keep it quiet. They were friends, you know, and Dad agreed. But Bill never paid a dime. He was called in to the meetings to see if he would ever pay anything, and he said that he couldn't. That's why Dad felt he had to accept the higher offer. The embezzlement had him strapped, and he couldn't bring himself to report Bill."

Max said, "So Pete's idea that he's owed money is nuts. I don't know if that will matter to him. He doesn't seem very lucid. But I'll go try to talk him out of this craziness. Have you got a flashlight?"

Bob said, "Yes—right on the porch. Be right back." When he returned, he handed Max a large flashlight. "Be careful."

As Max hurried back to the shed, she heard a siren in the distance. It occurred to her then that Pete's alibi for

Dutch's murder depended on two sleeping people. She was sure now that he had brought Donnie to town, dumped him in Dutch's car, and used the antenna to commit the murder. He was jealous of what he thought Donnie had and angry at how he thought he had been cheated. Those feelings had apparently molded his whole life. A tragedy.

She ducked in the door and, using the flashlight, moved as quickly as she could toward the back.

"Pete? It's Max. I need to talk to you and I'm by myself."

She heard mumbling but no clear answer, so she kept going.

Pete still held Donnie around the neck with his left arm, gun in his other hand. Chelsea sat on the ground, her knees up and her face buried in her arms.

"Stop right there," Pete said.

She stopped.

"How about the money?" Pete asked.

"We need more time. An hour isn't even long enough to get to town, get the money, and get back here." Max took a deep breath. "There's something else you should know, Pete—something we just found out. Your dad stole a lot of money from the company. That's why he didn't get a retirement package."

"You lie."

"No, the lawyer found documents, including a letter from your dad. Please let Donnie and Chelsea go, and w can work this out." She didn't know if there was a letter, but a white lie didn't matter at this point.

Chelsea raised her head and watched to see Pete's reaction.

"No, no, no—it's too late." He swung his head wildly, the gun waving precariously close to Donnie's head.

"How about just Chelsea? She has nothing to do with this."

He sighed, and then swung the gun toward the girl. "All right, get out of here."

Chelsea jumped to her feet and bolted around the other side of the shed. The sound of the siren reached inside the shed, and Pete swung the gun back toward her.

"You double-crossed me!"

Donnie moved so quickly that Max wasn't completely sure what happened. His right arm came up, knocking Pete's arm up as well, and the gun went flying. Donnie clung to the arm. Pete still had his left arm around Donnie's neck and Donnie fought to pull it away with his own left.

"Run, Max," Donnie yelled.

But she was so surprised that the moment passed, and when she saw Pete start to regain control over Donnie, she lunged at Pete's left arm and held on for all was worth. He was obviously stronger than either Donnie alone but not both of them together. He around, but they clung like crabs. Max knew losing her grip when she heard, "Hands up,

Sheriff Burns stood in a shooter's stance at the corner. Max and Donnie let go at the same time, causing Pete to fall back against the wall, hitting the back of his head. Max scrambled on hands and knees toward the sheriff, adrenalin overcoming the stabbing pain in her knees. Donnie dove for the gun and rolled out of the way.

It was over. The sheriff jerked Pete to his feet and cuffed his hands. Pete appeared dazed and gave no resistance. Max rolled over on her side and tried to catch her breath.

"Let me help you up." She looked up to see Donnie standing over her, hands outstretched. He too gasped for breath.

Chelsea had followed the sheriff and had been standing behind him. Now she rushed forward to help Max as well. She and Donnie got Max up, and Chelsea insisted that Max put one arm over her shoulders. Max hobbled along with aching knees and a sore shin, but they made it out of the building.

Everyone gathered around. Carol held Rosie back until Max could get seated on the patio. Janet hugged her husband and sobbed—something else the rest of the family had not seen since their wedding. The sheriff ushered Pete to his cruiser and told them he would be back later.

During the next hour, Max, Donnie and Chelsea shared the events in the shed in bits and pieces, trying to compose a coherent account. By the time the sheriff returned, Bob had picked up carryout from the Mexica restaurant in town, and Max was on her second glass of wine.

"The first order of business is to get that thing off your ankle," Sheriff Burns told Donnie. Once that was completed, he took the offered chair and held up his hands to fend off the barrage of questions.

"One at a time. First let me fill you in on what I've learned from Pete." He shifted in his chair and took a drink of iced tea provided by Carol. "He was apparently responsible for most of what's gone on. He admitted to bringing Donnie into town late Friday night—or actually, early Saturday morning—putting him in Dutch's car, and murdering Dutch, totally as a frame-up job. He, J.P Prentiss, and another friend concocted the float and drove it in the parade. They were not all asleep at the trailer like they said. And Pete's the one who locked your family in the plant. Donnie had mentioned the tour the night before."

Lil shook her head. "Hard to believe anyone would go to all of that work for a grudge."

"Plenty of people do, and he's not of sound mind," Max said. "He was like a crazy man when he was holding Donnie and threatening us."

The sheriff nodded. "I wouldn't be surprised if his ·ver uses that as a defense."

·ol related what they had just found out about the ement. "Pete has apparently been consumed all years with how he thought our family had life."

"Right," Burns said, "so the book Dutch was writing had nothing to do with it. We did find the manuscript, by the way, in his apartment and there is nothing derogatory about your family in it."

"That's a relief," Max said, ignoring Bob's amused expression. "What about the shots that hit my car yesterday?"

"That was Pete too. He had a shortcut back to his trailer. J.P. had called him and told him you were headed his way." He stood. "I guess that covers it and I need to get going. Any other questions?"

"I don't think so," Bob said. "Thank you, Sheriff."

After he left, Carol got up to refill iced tea glasses. "I'm so glad it's over. I just feel like this whole weekend was a disaster."

Max shook her head. "Stop beating yourself up. No way you and Annie could know any of this would happen. Besides, we might have all learned some lessons. This young lady—," she put her hand on Chelsea's shoulder, "was incredibly brave today. I was so proud of her."

Chelsea beamed. Max had a feeling no one had been proud of her lately, and for good reason. "Thank you. I should have done something more…"

"No, you shouldn't have. The guy was crazy. If you had done something, Donnie would probably be dead and maybe you too."

Donnie cleared his throat and leaned forward, elbows on knees and hands clasped. "I don't know what to say, exactly. I know I've been a spoiled brat and I'm going to try to do better." He nodded toward his wife. "Janet's going to help, and the first thing I'm going to do when we get home is join a twelve-step program. But thank you. I haven't deserved sisters like you."

Max said, "You've always said that. Only that you didn't deserve such *bad* sisters."

That brought a laugh and lightened the mood.

"Well, you're right. But we're going to head home." Donnie reverted to his smart-aleck persona. "Tell Annie the next time she wants to organize a reunion, maybe we should do it at a resort far away from here."

"Maybe you should organize the next one and you can do it wherever you want," Carol said, but gave him a hug.

Janet thanked them, too—another first—and Donnie offered to drop Chelsea off at Annie's.

Soon, just Bob and Carol, Max, and Lil were left on the patio.

Max shifted in her chair. "One question the sheriff didn't answer--and I'm not going to ask him--is who was in Dutch's apartment when Tess and I took the manuscript back. No reason for it to be Pete. Someone who was worried about that book."

"We'll probably never know," Lil said.

Carol's phone rang. Her side of the conversation was brief--mostly okays, yeses, and a thank you. As she put the phone away, she looked at the others in disbelief.

"That was Her Honor the Mayor. Max, you and Chelsea must have wowed her. She's talked to most of the council members, and they're very interested in the community center idea. They're going to check out the legalities and they'll be in touch."

Max was shocked. "She was about as enthusiastic as a fish about to be caught. Chelsea will be astounded. We both thought it was a dead end."

"So what's your plans?" Carol asked Max and Lil.

"I thought maybe we'd stay several more days so we could have a nice long visit," Max said. She laughed at Carol's slightly panicked expression. "Just kidding. If my knees are okay, we'll take off in the morning. You know what they say about fish and company."

Thank You...

For taking your time to share Max and Lil's adventures. Just as the sound of a tree falling in the forest depends on hearers, a book only matters if it has readers. Please consider sharing your thoughts with other readers in a review on Amazon and/or Goodreads. Or email me at karen.musser.nortman@gmail.com.

My website at http://www.karenmussernortman.com provides updates on my books, my blog, and photos of our for-real camping trips. Sign up on my website for my email list and get a free download of *Bats and Bones*.

To my Beta readers, Ginge, Elaine, Marcia, and Butch, thank you for all of the great catches and suggestions. To Stew Hodge, thanks for the advice on guns. And to all of my readers, especially my advance reader team, words are not enough.

The inspiration for the Mystery Sisters was memories of my Great Aunt Mary, who taught phys ed in Missouri until she was in her seventies. She owned a Studebaker and during the summer would drive up to southern Minnesota, pick up my grandmother, and off they'd go to California or Connecticut or some other exotic place (in my teenaged mind). My cousin says they argued constantly, but they made trip after trip. I stole the names of the sisters (but not the personalities) from three of my youngest aunts--the ones who were between my and my parents generation. They were the 'cool' aunts—young and hip. And they were a great example to us all.

Other Books by the Author

The award-winning Frannie Shoemaker Campground Mysteries:

Bats and Bones: (An IndieBRAG Medallion honoree) Frannie and Larry Shoemaker are retirees who enjoy weekend camping with their friends in state parks. They anticipate the usual hiking, campfires, good food, and interesting side trips among the bluffs of beautiful Bat Cave State Park for the long Fourth of July weekend—until a dead body turns up. Confined in the campground and surrounded by strangers, Frannie is drawn into the investigation. Frannie's persistence and curiosity helps authorities sort through the possible suspects and motives, but almost ends her new sleuth career—and her life—for good.

The Blue Coyote: (An IndieBRAG Medallion honoree and a 2013 Chanticleer CLUE finalist) Frannie and Larry Shoemaker love taking their grandchildren, Sabet and Joe, camping with them. But at Bluffs State Park, Frannie finds herself worrying more than usual about their safety, and when another young girl disappears from the campground in broad daylight, her fears increase. The fun of a bike ride, a flea market, marshmallow guns, and a storyteller are quickly overshadowed. Accusations against Larry and her add to the cloud over their heads.

Peete and Repeat: (An IndieBRAG Medallion honoree, 2013 Chanticleer CLUE finalist, and 2014 Chanticleer Mystery and Mayhem finalist) A biking and camping trip to southeastern Minnesota turns into double trouble for Frannie Shoemaker and her friends as she deals with a canoeing mishap and a couple of bodies. Strange happenings in the campground, the nearby nature learning center, and an old power plant complicate the suspect pool and Frannie tries to stay out of it--really--but what can she do?

The Lady of the Lake: (An IndieBRAG Medallion honoree, 2014 Chanticleer CLUE finalist) A trip down memory lane is fine if you don't stumble on a body. Frannie Shoemaker and her friends camp at Old Dam Trail State Park near one of Donna Nowak's childhood homes. They take in the county fair, reminisce at a Fifties-Sixties dance, and check out old hangouts. But the present intrudes when a body surfaces. Donna becomes the focus of the investigation and Frannie wonders if the police shouldn't be looking closer at the victim's many enemies. A traveling goddess worshipper, a mystery writer and the Sisters on the Fly add color to the campground.

To Cache a Killer: Geocaching isn't supposed to be about finding dead bodies. But when retiree, Frannie Shoemaker go camping, standard definitions don't apply. A weekend in a beautiful state park in Iowa buzzes with fund-raising events, a search for Ninja turtles, a bevy of suspects, and lots of great food. But are the campers in the wrong place at the wrong time once too often?

The Space Invader: A cozy/thriller mystery! The starry skies over New Mexico, the "Land of Enchantment," may hold secrets of their own. The Shoemakers and the Ferraros, on an extended camping trip, find themselves picking up a souvenir they don't want and taking side trips they didn't plan on.

Real Actors, Not People: Frannie Shoemaker and her friends go camping to get away from the real world. So they are surprised and dismayed to find their wilderness campground the production site of a new 'reality' show-- Celebrity Campout. Reality intrudes on their week in the form of accidents, nature, and even murder. They handle the situation with their usual humor, compassion, and mystery solving, because...camping can be murder.

We are NOT Buying a Camper! A prequel to the Frannie Shoemaker Campground Mysteries. Frannie and Larry Shoemaker have busy jobs, two teenagers, and plenty of other demands on their time and sanity. Larry's sister and brother-in-law pester them to try camping for relaxation-- time to sit back, enjoy nature, and catch up on naps. After all, what could go wrong? Join Frannie as "RV there yet?" becomes "RV crazy?" and she learns that going back to nature doesn't necessarily mean a simpler life.

A Campy Christmas: A Holiday novella. The Shoemakers and Ferraros plan to spend Christmas in Texas and then take a camping trip through the Southwest. But those plans are stopped cold when they hit a rogue ice storm in Missouri and they end up snowbound in a campground. And that's just the beginning. Includes recipes and winter camping tips.

Happy Camper Tips and Recipes: All of the tips and recipes from the first four Frannie Shoemaker books in one convenient paperback or Kindle version that you can keep in your camping supplies.

THE TIME TRAVEL TRAILER SERIES

The Time Travel Trailer: (An IndieBRAG Medallion honoree, 2015 Chanticleer Paranormal First-in-Category winner) A 1937 vintage camper trailer half hidden in weeds catches Lynne McBriar's eye when she is visiting an elderly friend Ben. Ben eagerly sells it to her and she just as eagerly embarks on a restoration. But after each remodel, sleeping in the trailer lands Lynne and her daughter Dinah in a previous decade—exciting, yet frightening. Glimpses of their home town and ancestors fifty or sixty years earlier is exciting and also offers some clues to the mystery of Ben's lost love. But when Dinah makes a trip on her own, separating herself from her mother by decades, Lynne has never known such fear. It is a trip that may upset the future if Lynne and her estranged husband can't team up to bring their daughter back.

Trailer on the Fly: How many of us have wished at some time or other we could go back in time and change an action or a decision or just take back something that was said? But it is what it is. There is no rewind, reboot, delete key or any other trick to change the past, right?
Lynne McBriar can. She bought a 1937 camper that turned out to be a time portal. And when she meets a young woman who suffers from serious depression over the loss of a close friend ten years earlier, she has the power to do something about it. And there is no reason not to use that power. Right?

Trailer, Get Your Kicks!: Lynne McBriar swore her vintage trailer would stay in a museum where it would be safe from further time travel. But when a museum in Texas wants to borrow it, she determines that she must deliver it herself. Her husband Kurt convinces her to take it along Route 66 for research he is doing. What starts out as a family vacation soon turns deadly, and ends with a romance unworn by time. Travel can be dangerous any time, but when your trip involves the Time Travel Trailer, who knows where (or when) you will end up?

<<<<>>>>

About the Author

Karen Musser Nortman is the author of the Frannie Shoemaker Campground cozy mystery series, including several BRAGMedallion honorees. After previous incarnations as a secondary social studies teacher (22 years) and a test developer (18 years), she returned to her childhood dream of writing a novel. The Frannie Shoemaker Campground Mysteries came out of numerous 'round the campfire' discussions, making up answers to questions raised by the peephole glimpses one gets into the lives of fellow campers. Where did those people disappear to for the last two days? What kinds of bones are in this fire pit? Why is that woman wearing heels to the shower house?

Karen and her husband Butch originally tent camped when their children were young and switched to a travel trailer when sleeping on the ground lost its romantic adventure. They take frequent weekend jaunts with friends to parks in Iowa and surrounding states, plus occasional longer trips. Entertainment on these trips has ranged from geocaching and hiking/biking to barbecue contests, balloon fests, and buck skinners' rendezvous.

Sign up for Karen's email list at www.karenmussernortman.com and receive a free ereader download of *Bats and Bones*.

Made in United States
Troutdale, OR
10/24/2024